D...
THE DALEKS:
MISSION

DOCTOR WHO
THE DALEKS' MASTERPLAN – PART I
MISSION TO THE UNKNOWN

based on the BBC television series by Terry Nation
and Dennis Spooner by arrangement with BBC Books,
a division of BBC Enterprises Ltd

JOHN PEEL

Number 141 in the
Target Doctor Who Library

TARGET

A TARGET BOOK
published by
the Paperback Division of
W H Allen & Co Plc

A Target Book
Published in 1989
By the Paperback Division of
W H Allen & Co Plc
Sekforde House, 175/9 St John Street, London EC1V 4LL

The BBC producer of Verity Lambert
The director was Douglas Camfield
The role of the Doctor was played by William Hartnell

Printed and bound in Great Britain by
Cox & Wyman Ltd, Reading

ISBN 0 426 20343 7

Contents

1

The Toppled Towers Of Ilium

Smoke filled the city as the invading Greeks torched every building that they could set alight. The night was bright with the dancing flames, proclaiming the final end of the Trojan War. Ten long, frustrating years for the Greeks were over – now, thanks to the brilliance of Odysseus, they were inside the city of their most hated foes! Their anger spilled out with the blood of the screaming, fleeing Trojans. Berserk now, the invading troops ran through the streets and houses killing, looting and burning.

In the thoroughfares, small knots of Trojan soldiers tried to hold back the flood, at the same time gathering together what women and children they could. Fighting a desperate rearguard action, they struggled to escape the doomed Troy, and make it to safety on the plains.

One small group ran neither forward to loot and pillage nor back to flee the city. An old man, in loose Greek robes, with long silver hair and a silver-tipped cane struggled to help a young girl. She was almost borne to her knees under the weight of a warrior in Greek garb – the short leather skirt, the copper breastplate and the thonged sandals. His helmet was long discarded, and his handsome face was pale. The section of his clothing below the breastplate was dark with his life-blood. What was most strange about the elfin, dark-haired girl helping to drag him through the smoke was that she was a Trojan, dressed as a serving girl from the palace of King Priam himself.

'Here,' the Doctor called, gesturing to a small ante-room of the palace. 'Katarina, we must take Steven in here.'

Though she nodded and helped with the struggle to get

Steven into the blazing building, Katarina could not understand why the old man wanted his friend to be helped into a room that in moments would be an inferno. Still, the Doctor was perhaps Zeus in disguise – did not the gods often walk upon the Earth? To him, the flames might not be hot, but cool and refreshing. To her? Well, she must trust. Ahead of them, she could make out the strange, tall blue box that had so puzzled King Priam when it had been brought to him. No one had been able to open it.

Trying vainly to brush away the smoke that filled everywhere, the Doctor managed to pull the key from his clothing. Eyes streaming, he fitted it into the lock and turned it.

The TARDIS doors swung inwards. The Doctor, unable to speak without coughing, gestured for Katarina to help him get Steven within. Still uncomprehending, but trusting, she did so. As soon as they were inside, the Doctor abandoned both his companions and hurried over to the console. He triggered the door switch, and the double doors swung closed behind them. He coughed again, then smiled briefly. 'Ah! Fresh air, at last. Now we can breathe.'

Katarina was staggered by the size of the room that they were in: this was no small chest as it had seemed from the outside, but a temple annexe, at least thirty feet across! Lights blazed on the white walls that looked like polished stone. An altar stood in the centre of the room, over which the Doctor brooded, moving sticks and touching coloured baubles. What could he be doing? Suddenly the centre of the altar began to rise and fall, and a terrible noise, the baying of Cerberus, guardian hound of the Underworld, began. Katarina fell to her knees and hid her face in terror.

Oblivious, the Doctor finished setting the controls. 'The sooner we are away from this barbaric period,' he muttered, 'the better I shall like it.' He glanced down at his clothing in disgust. 'And the sooner I am properly attired again . . .' Finally, he remembered his companions, and turned to them. Steven was on the floor, very still, and that silly handmaiden, Katarina, was all in a bundle. How could he have let Vicki talk him into taking this girl along to help with Steven? But Vicki had insisted on staying with that young whipper-snapper . . . what was his name? Ah, Troilus! That was it. Love! It did silly things to humans, especially the females. Why, it had even affected his own granddaughter not that long ago . . .

Heaving himself out of his reverie, the Doctor hurried over to Katarina and Steven. 'Oh, do get up,' he snapped crossly at the Trojan girl. 'Give me a hand with Steven. We had better get him to bed, and get this armour off him. I must see what shape that wound is in.'

Katarina looked up, timorously. 'Is this your temple?'

'My what? What are you talking about?'

She gestured about the room. 'This is your temple,' she said, more firmly.

'It is nothing of the kind,' the Doctor replied crossly. 'It's my ship.'

'This is no ship,' Katarina laughed. 'Where are the sails? Where are the oarsmen? No, this is your temple, and we are journeying through the Underworld to the Place of Perfection.'

What a stupid child! The Doctor sighed, realizing that she couldn't help it. Science was unknown in her culture, and she was doing what she could to try to make sense of what was happening to her. 'Yes, well, whatever you like,' he said, brusquely. 'Just give me a hand to get Steven to a bed, will you?'

Together, they half-carried, half-dragged him through the far doors and into his own room in the TARDIS. Once Steven was stretched out on the bed, the Doctor looked him over. He seemed very weak and pale, and was having trouble breathing. 'Can you get this silly plate off him?' the Doctor asked Katarina.

'Of course. I am a handmaid in the palace of Priam of Troy. I know of the accoutrements of war.'

'Well, stop boasting and just do it, child.'

Katarina set to work, and within moments had the fastenings undone. Gently, she removed the breastplate and set it down. Steven's tunic was soaked in blood. She tenderly moved the cloth aside, so as not to hurt him further. 'I shall need water,' she said, 'if I am to help your priest. The wound has bitten deep.'

The Doctor nodded, and hurried off to get warm water for her. Whatever her faults, she did seem to have more than a nodding acquaintance with sword-wounds. As soon as he had the water ready, he hurried back with it. Katarina had meanwhile started to clean out the wound, using the cloths at hand. Without a word, the Doctor handed her the bowl of warm water. Katarina, in her element now, continued her task. The Doctor left her, and went to his medicine chest.

It was sorely depleted. He had intended to fill it on many of his trips, but had become so easily side-tracked. A bandage, some gauze and a little antiseptic cream was the best that he could manage. Hurrying back, he saw that Katarina had sponged off the blood that had covered Steven's wound. It was a nasty gash in his side, but had luckily missed penetrating anything vital. The Doctor didn't like the red colour of the skin about the wound, or Steven's laboured breathing. He seriously doubted that the Trojan sword that had cut into his young companion had been sterile. By now, millions of germs could have infected Steven. The Doctor elbowed Katarina aside, and started to apply his makeshift dressing.

'I have seen such a wound many times,' Katarina offered. 'It is invariably fatal. Your priest will die. I am sorry for you, but at least we shall take him down to the Underworld in your temple.'

'Oh, do stop that!' the Doctor snapped. 'You're no Florence Nightingale, and that's for certain! All he needs are some antibiotics to combat the toxins, and he'll be fine.'

Katarina regarded him uncomprehendingly. 'I do not understand your words,' she confessed. 'Do you mean that you can cure even such a mortal wound?'

'Of course. Ah, well, that is – I can with proper medication. What we need is to find a world and time which is sufficiently sophisticated to have developed such medication.' Seeing her blank expression, the Doctor simplified his explanation to suit her level of understanding. 'My temple passes through many worlds on its journey. On some of them, there exist the herbs I need to cure my priest. I must simply seek help.'

At last, Katarina smiled. 'Ah! You seek out the secrets of the Underworld, the fabled plants that give immortal life! With those, you can save the life of Steven!'

The Doctor nodded. 'Whatever you say,' he agreed. 'You stay here and nurse him as best you can. I shall try to steer my – ah – temple to some suitable spot. If we cannot find the right . . . herbs, I am very much afraid that Steven will die.'

2

The Screaming Jungle

An eldritch scream rent the air, the sound of a hunting animal having succeeded in its quest. Garvey's eyes snapped open, and he cast about for several seconds. He could see nothing but the vast, impersonal jungle that covered almost all of the land area of this planet. Tall trees sought the sky, while huge creepers tried to tie them to the ground. Shrubs, bushes, grasses and worse were scattered about the trees. Every now and again, something rustled through the undergrowth, or there was a movement in the branches. In all the time that he had been here, Garvey had seen no animal life, however. Any creatures in this nightmare forest were too cautious to expose themselves to view. All Garvey or his companions had seen were the endless plants. Worst of all were the ever-present, beautiful-seeming orchid trees. Tall, multi-coloured growths, they gave forth delightful scents – and spat deadly poison on to anyone foolish enough to get too close to them. The plants were carnivorous, and once their prey had thrashed in agony and died, the plant would slowly lower its bell over the carcass and begin to feed. Garvey had even seen one variety of the orchids that shot out a jet of fire – a thick liquid that burst into flames on contact with the air. The liquid would stick to its victim and burn them horribly to death.

The jungle was at its worst when it showed its most lovely face. Bright colours, delectable scents and cheerful appearance meant that the plants were lures.

But they had heard far more. The jungle held a background chatter of noises – perhaps simply territorial cries, mates calling to one another and baby creatures calling out in puzzlement at the world in which they found themselves.

Garvey doubted this: he believed that the cries were of death and impending death, of hunters and victims. He had become convinced that very soon his voice would echo through this nightmare forest.

He realized that he was panting in fear again, and made a heroic effort to calm down. Sweat plastered his face and the palms of his hands. Nervously, he rubbed them on his dark uniform to dry them. Once, on Earth, he had been considered handsome, but now his face was pinched with constant terror, etched by the rivulets of sweaty fear and dirtied by constantly being buried in the undergrowth when he hid from – what?

Now that he was awake, he began to wonder. Why was he here? What was he doing? What had happened . . .

The pain began, building swiftly behind his eyes, burning at his brain. With a hollow cry he collapsed, gripping his temples, squeezing, trying to relieve the terrible pain. He threw back his head, but even in his agony, his fear reminded him to make as little noise as possible, and he stayed silent. After long, stabbing seconds, the pain began to ebb, and he could let go of his head. Something had come back to him, and he now knew what he must do.

He reached for his belt, and unbuckled his pistol. With practised ease, he checked the remaining charges, and then set the weapon to its highest beam. A smile that would have done credit to some demon from the pits of Hell swept across his face. 'I remember,' he muttered to himself. 'Remember . . . I must kill. Must kill . . . kill . . .'

Just over a mile from Garvey, one alien artefact stood in a small clearing of its own creation. The small scout ship had swung down over Kembel as it had approached, and then this site had been selected for a landing. The rockets that had slowed the ship to a landing had burnt away the vegetation for several hundred yards around. Despite this, the jungle was starting even now to edge in closer, eager to fill up this gap in itself.

The scout ship was small, designed for in-system flight and not inter-planetary hops. It was barely large enough to contain its three passengers or crew and several days' supplies for them. The rest of the ship was the reaction drive, and it was this that was causing the problems. The final two members of this expedition were standing by a small hole in the hull. The plate they had removed lay on the scorched ground beside them.

Marc Cory was holding the tool chest, and trying to see what his companion was doing. Cory was lean, tall and dark, in a good-looking way. He was just a shade on the right side of thirty, and possessed what seemed to be a vast indifference to the Universe in general. Unlike Garvey, Cory was not terrified of Kembel; it was simply another world of the many he had visited in the past few years. Some had been worse than this, though most had been better. Kembel was just a job to Cory, one to be accomplished swiftly, so he could move on to the next.

His companion, currently head and shoulders into the cavity in the ship's hull, was the captain-pilot, Gordon Lowery. A gentler, cheerier man than Cory, Lowery also could have cared less about Kembel. He was a born spacer, eager to get off worlds with their unpleasant gravity and back into free space, where he belonged. At the moment, this was impossible, so he blamed the man responsible. 'Why you wanted to land on this planet I'll *never* know,' he grumbled over his shoulder. 'It's getting on my nerves.' To punctuate his comment, there was another ululating squeal from the jungle. 'I hate to think what kind of animal makes a noise like that,' he added. 'And you notice something? They're getting closer.' Hearing just a grunt from Cory, Lowery stuck his head out of the panel. 'I'll tell you one thing – I don't want to be around when whatever-it-is arrives. Hand me that wrench, will you?'

Cory peered into the box of gadgets, almost all of which looked as alien to him as the landscape. On a hunch, he pulled out what he considered to be a wrench and offered it to Lowery. Lowery scowled, waved it aside, and pulled a different instrument from the box. His head and arms vanished back into the hatchway. Cory shrugged. 'So, how's it going?' he asked, conversationally.

'Slow,' came the reply. 'The flareback melted some of the retaining heads, and all we've got is solid lumps of Tarnium instead of precision contacts, I've got to get them free and replace them.'

'Is there time for me to look around?'

Lowery's head popped out again; with a distinctly angry expression on it. 'Look, if we don't lift off in the next hour, we'll miss the rendezvous with the freighter. If we're not there, they'll assume that we aren't coming. They won't wait.'

'You'll make it, Lowery.'

'I'm doing the best I can,' Lowery yelled back, waving the wrench about threateningly. He didn't like passengers who made him damage his ship – especially ones who seemed indifferent to the problems. 'I didn't want to touch down on this lousy planet anyway.'

'Let's not start that again,' Cory suggested. 'Just get on with the work, eh?'

For a moment, Lowery looked all set to use the wrench on Cory, but he finally bent back to his task. Cory set down the box of tools, and stared off to the south. 'Where the devil is Garvey?' he asked, rhetorically. 'He should have been back by now.'

Lowery answered anyhow. 'He'll be here for take-off – *if* we take off. Screwdriver!' He held out his hand, and gestured. Cory hazarded another guess in the toolbox, and this time was correct. The instrument vanished into the hole.

With Cory's attention diverted from the jungle, he failed to see the rustling of the leaves as Garvey peered out at the ship. The lone man smiled his evil grin again, and stared at the ship and the two men working on it. He clutched at his pistol, and the haze descended over his brain again. What was it he had to do? Ah, yes! *Kill* . . .

He lurched unsteadily to his feet, and moved quietly into the open. Then he slipped about the clearing until the bulk of the scout ship was between him and his prey . . .

There was a loud snapping sound, and Lowery re-emerged from the cavity in the hull, holding a piece of melted metal. 'Look at that!' he exclaimed. 'It's useless.' He flung it with considerable force towards the jungle. 'Get me a spare, will you?' Cory assumed that it was one of the retaining whatevers that the pilot had been complaining about, and started to rummage about in the toolbox for a replacement. 'Not in there,' Lowery said, 'in the ship's store.'

Nodding, Cory clambered inside the small ship. Lowery set to work on the other lump of fused metal. Lost in his work, he failed to see or hear the approaching form of Garvey. Garvey, on the other hand, had an excellent view of Lowery. He smiled his wicked smile again, and raised his pistol for a shot into the back of his unsuspecting comrade.

'Cory, don't bother!' Lowery yelled out. 'Spares aren't going to do us any good. This thing's spattered all over the valve linkages.'

Garvey's face was sweating, but his hand was steady. He began to squeeze the trigger, slowly . . .

At the sound of the blaster, Lowery spun about, in time to see the brief flare that silhouetted Garvey's body, and to hear the final scream that escaped the man's lips. As Garvey fell, face down, Lowery could see Cory standing in the hatchway, his pistol at the ready. Lowery ran to Garvey, and turned him over. It was quite obvious that the man was dead.

Stricken, Lowery looked up at Cory, who had merely jumped lightly down to the ground. He stood there, impassive, as though killing a man was merely all in a day's work. 'You . . . you've killed him. *Killed* Garvey!'

Cory replaced his pistol in its holster with apparent uninterest. 'It was him or you.'

The lack of remorse from Cory was too much for Lowery. He launched himself at the other. 'You sadistic swine!' he screamed. 'You didn't give him a chance! You just shot him down like an animal. *You just murdered him!*' Had Lowery been a trifle wiser, he would have known better than to attack Cory. Instead of his hands connecting with Cory's neck, his face connected with Cory's swinging fist.

16

Lowery was thrown back, and hit the ground with considerable force.

The breath was knocked out of him, and both his back and chin ached horribly. He could do nothing but watch as Cory moved lithely to Garvey's body. The man pulled open one of the fallen eyelids, nodded, and then started to examine Garvey's skin. Finally, just below and behind the right ear he found what he was looking for. Carefully, he removed the object from the skin, and held it out towards Lowery. 'Varga thorn,' he explained.

It meant nothing to Lowery, who was beginning to get mobile again. 'Varga thorn?' he echoed. Carefully, he clambered to his feet and crossed to Cory, moving slowly. He had no desire to run into another of those punches. He reached out to take the thorn.

'Careful,' Cory warned him. 'Don't prick yourself with it, or you'll end up the way that Garvey did – I'd have to kill you, too.'

The pilot whipped back his hand. 'What do you mean?'

Before Cory could reply, there came another long, mournful howl from the jungle. Cory glanced about, then gestured upwards. 'Let's go into the ship. I'd better explain.'

Lowery paused for just a moment to look down at his dead friend. Shaking his head, he reflected that Cory had better have a very good explanation for what he had done – or, somehow, he'd find a way to kill the man. He followed Cory up into the ship, and shut the hatch behind him, closing off the nightmares of Kembel for a short while.

A very short while.

Garvey's body lay by the ship, still and stark against the dark earth. A slight twitch shook the hand, then another. The fingers began to flex slowly, and then clenched. Finally, the hand moved to help support what had once been Garvey. Over the back of the hand was a covering of long, white hairs. Interspersed among the hairs were the slim, deadly varga thorns – only these were not stuck into the skin. They were growing *out* of it . . .

★ ★ ★

17

The inside of the control room was cluttered, since space was at a premium. Three acceleration couches lined one wall. The airlock by which Cory and Lowery had entered filled a second, and Lowery's instrumentation took up most of the remaining room. For a moment, Cory stared at the dead panels, then turned to face Lowery. 'There are some facts you're entitled to know,' he stated. 'I hadn't intended to tell you anything, but Garvey's death has changed all of that.'

From the tone of Cory's voice, Lowery could tell that the man was far more worried than he might appear. Curiosity dawned within him. 'What sort of things?'

In reply, Cory fished out a small document from his breast pocket, and handed it over to Lowery. The pilot scanned the first page and blinked at what it said. Now he knew why Cory was so self-composed and efficient with his fists and gun. 'Special Security Service,' he muttered.

'That's right,' Cory agreed. 'The rest of the document gives me the authority to enlist the aid of any person, civilian or military.' He paused to give an ironic half-smile. 'You were just enlisted. From here on, you follow my orders to the letter.'

'Cory . . . I don't understand.' All thoughts of revenge for Garvey's death had fled now, replaced by a whole mountain of questions. 'You'd better give me some details.'

'All right.' Cory moved to sit on one of the couches, and gestured for Lowery to join him. Then he continued: 'Did you ever hear of the Daleks?'

'Daleks?' Lowery looked puzzled. 'Who hasn't? They invaded the Earth a couple of times, and were beaten back. Every schoolkid knows about that. Haven't heard much about them since the Movellan Wars – oh, a thousand years or more now, I should think.'

'That's right. Well, just because they haven't been active in the Galaxy for a long time doesn't mean that they've just been sitting around. In the last five hundred years, they've gained control of over seventy planets in the Andromeda Galaxy, and some forty more in Miros.'

Lowery shrugged. 'I don't see why that should concern us. They're both millions of light years away from us.'

'Yeah, that's what we thought. Plenty of time to worry when they came closer. But about a week ago, we had a report from the captain of a freighter out in this region. His navigator had spotted a ship he couldn't identify. He saw it very briefly, but gave us a very good description.'

'And?' prompted Lowery, afraid he knew what was coming.

'What he described was a Dalek ship.'

Outside, Garvey had finally managed to get both hands under himself, and pushed down hard. As he rose, his legs came back to life, with the same spasmodic, jerky motions that his hands had shown. His trousers had ruptured, and through the tears, white hairs and thorns stuck out. His shoes split, and fell off. His tunic tore, and the cloth hung in clumps. His head was unrecognizable now. All over his body were the same thick white hairs and the varga thorns jutting out at all angles.

Garvey was no longer a human being.

His hands had vanished, instead having become wood-like branches, sticking out from the main stem. His feet had become roots, thick, and gnarled and long. Instead of sinking into the ground, though, they supported the varga plant that had once been a laughing, cheerful person named Garvey. Unsteadily, the plant lurched, attempting to find its balance. One woody 'leg' at a time, it moved slowly towards the scout ship, a single thought fixed in what passed for its brain:

Kill . . .

Throwing down the microphone in disgust, Cory shook his head. 'Dead!' he grunted. 'You sure we can't repair the ship?'

'Not a chance,' Lowery replied, bitterly. 'There was too much damage from the molten metal in the circuits. If I had a full repair bay, maybe . . . and if I had wings, I could fly. Listen, do you think that the Daleks have set up some kind of a base on Kembel, then?'

'Could be. This is the most hostile planet in the Galaxy. Virtually everybody avoids it, and it seemed to me that if you added this fact to the sighting of the Dalek ship, this place could make an ideal base for any kind of secret preparations that the Daleks might want to make. That's why we came here.'

Lowery rubbed his chin thoughtfully. 'Did you tell anyone else about this hunch of yours?'

'No one,' Cory answered, disgusted with himself. 'Not even your commander. I just asked for a couple of men and a small ship, without telling him why. He couldn't turn me down.' He waved the documents that Lowery had handed back over, then put them away. 'Even SSS don't know why I'm here. I tend to have a reputation for taking long shots.'

'Then why are you now telling me?'

'Because of this.' Cory held out the thorn again. 'A thorn from a varga plant. It's a strange creature that's part animal, part vegetable. Looks a bit like a cactus, with poisoned spines. The toxin attacks the brain, overwhelming all rational thoughts and replacing them with an unreasoning desire to kill. Eventually, the poison seeps through the victim's body, and it starts to metabolize them. The person is gradually changed into a varga plant.'

Thinking about this, Lowery shuddered in disgust. He imagined his own body being infected, then being stolen from him as the varga started to grow within . . . 'Yeah, but . . . what's that got to do with the Daleks?'

'The only place that vargas grow naturally is on the Dalek home world of Skaro. If the vargas are here, then it makes sense that the Daleks are here, too.'

Deeper in the jungle, a small city occupied a clearing. Half-hidden by the trees, the small scout had missed seeing it by only a couple of miles as it came down. The buildings were all made from metal and glass, and were clustered around approximately half of a circular landing field. The field held berths for about twenty ships, though only two of these were currently occupied, both by Dalek saucers.

Within the base and overlooking this landing strip, the main control room was a hive of activity. Low-level lighting was quite sufficient for the Daleks, whose visual equipment, enhanced by computers, was far more acute than that of other species. Dozens of the gun-metal blue and silver Daleks busied themselves at their tasks – monitoring equipment, tracking stations, life-support, and a number of further computer screens. Around the room, below the large window that opened on to the field and the jungle beyond, a narrow platform circled the room.

A low, pulsing tone, like a vast electronic heart-beat, pervaded the whole city. For a brief moment, a higher-pitched, two-tone signal filled the control room. The Daleks on duty there turned their eye-sticks expectantly towards the main entrance. After a pause, the door hissed open, and the Black Dalek glided into the room.

The Black Dalek's eye-stick swivelled about, taking in all of the details. It had recently arived on Kembel, sent by the Dalek Prime from Skaro to oversee the operation in person. With satisfaction, it noted that everything appeared to be progressing well. 'I will receive your reports,' it grated. 'Space monitor control.'

The monitor Dalek moved slightly forwards to identify itself. 'The emissaries from the seven planets are all on their way, and will arrive on schedule.'

'Then the conference will begin at first sun,' the Black Dalek replied. 'Security report.'

A second Dalek edged forwards. 'Security patrols have located the alien spacecraft monitored landing on Kembel. Our patrol will reach it shortly.'

'The ship and its occupants must be totally destroyed!' the Black Dalek ordered. 'There must be no report on our work here. Destroy them!'

'It will be done.' The security leader glanced down at the panels. The patrol was almost in position now . . .

3

Extermination!

The night was drawing in about them both. The air was cold, and even in his thermal uniform, Cory felt cold. He suspected that the chill was internal, and held his pistol at the ready. The sounds from the jungle were wearing at his nerves, but what bothered him the most was the fact that they hadn't been able to find Garvey's body outside the ship. Had some animal, emboldened by hunger, snatched it? Or had something worse happened?

Movement in the bushes caught his attention, and he glided out to investigate. In the dim starlight, he could make out three white shapes standing by the edge of the trees. *Vargas!* They stood together, swaying slightly, though there was no breeze. Grimly, Cory turned back towards the ship. He steeled himself, and heard what he had expected.

One of the vargas lurched, and moved a pace closer.

Lowery was bent over the small framework near the scout ship that he was creating. A signal rocket, about six feet long, lay beside him as he worked to assemble a short launch ramp for it. The cone of the rocket was open and empty. Hearing Cory returning, Lowery called over his shoulder: 'Anything out there?'

'Vargas,' Cory answered, coldly. 'They're closing in.'

'Closing in?' Lowery echoed in alarm, looking up at the impassive agent. 'You mean they can move?'

'Very slowly. They use their roots to drag themselves forwards. One way of getting at their food supplies. How long will you be with that rescue beacon?'

'It's almost finished.'

'Good.' Cory glanced about. 'I don't know how long

we've got. The Daleks must know we're here by now. They'll be coming to look for us.'

'I still think you're jumping to conclusions,' Lowery protested, clutching at straws. 'Just because these . . . varga things grow here doesn't prove that the Daleks are here also.'

'Take my word for it. They're here.'

'Couldn't the vargas have grown here naturally?' At Cory's glance of withering scorn, Lowery said frantically: 'Well, it's possible, isn't it? Parallel evolution, that sort of thing? Maybe even transplanted somehow?'

'No. They were developed in Dalek laboratories. Daleks use them because they grow great natural protection. They feed on rotting flesh, and kill to get that flesh. With the vargas about, the Daleks don't have to be quite so careful themselves. Now stop asking silly questions and get on with that rescue beacon.'

'All right, all right!' Lowery snapped, returning to work with redoubled haste. He had learned all about the Daleks in history classes at school, and their malevolence towards all other life-forms was well ingrained in him. Varga plants were bad enough to face, but if the Daleks were really also here . . .

The four Daleks of the patrol halted in unison. One of them had a small device built into its arm-stick that looked like a compass. It moved about slightly, to verify the readings, then turned to its companions. 'Perceptor readings indicate alien spacecraft close by. We will move in on it from two directions.'

Two of the Daleks moved off to the east, chorusing: 'We obey.' The leader and the final Dalek circled to the west. Their objective was now almost within striking distance.

Unaware how close their enemies were, Lowery and Cory still worked with feverish haste. Actually, it was Lowery who was working, and Cory was getting nervous now, unable to help in matters of rocketry. 'You're sure this thing will work?' he asked, again.

'Sure. It's standard safety equipment on all scouts. You just record your message on the cassette, and insert it into the capsule. I'll make sure that it gets launched safely into a high orbit. The transmitters cut in as soon as the capsule is in stable orbit. Simple.'

Cory wished it were that simple. 'With what we now know about the Daleks, we've got to be picked up.'

'Well, it's tuned to the SSS special frequency you told me about. If they're monitoring for a call, then they'll get it loud and strong.'

'All we have to do is to stay alive till they get here,' Cory muttered, half to himself. Kembel was not an easy planet to stay alive on at the best of times; with the vargas and the Daleks here as well, it might just turn out to be impossible . . .

Both men became aware of a growing noise in the night sky. The looked upwards, only to see something huge moving across the sky. Lights on the craft flickered and pulsed; bathing the two men in coloured shadows. The ship passed overhead at a slow speed, rumbling, spinning, and then vanishing over the forest.

Lowery let out his breath, hardly even aware that he had been holding it. 'That's the biggest spaceship I've ever seen,' he said, stunned. 'It's like nothing we've got.'

'It's from an outer galaxy,' Cory informed him.

'Then what the devil is it doing here on a God-forsaken planet like this?'

'I don't know.' Cory would dearly have loved to follow the ship, which was obviously heading for the Dalek base on Kembel, but he didn't dare. The Dalek patrols in that direction were certain to intercept them if they tried. 'But I'll tell you one thing. Something very big is happening here. You can bet your life that the Daleks are up to something that might even place our entire Galaxy in danger . . .'

Two of the patrol Daleks paused as the ship hurtled over their heads, aiming for a touchdown at the base in the jungle.

'The ship from the planet Gearon,' the first observed.

'The beginning of the alliance,' the second added. Together, they then continued their approach to the alien intruders' ship.

With a sigh of satisfaction, Lowery laid down his tools. The framework about the message rocket was now completed, and all that was missing was the warning itself. 'All done,' he announced. 'Give me the recorder and I'll tape the message.' When Cory didn't answer, Lowery nudged him.

'Ssh!' the agent said, urgently. Lowery jumped to his feet, and followed Cory's gaze into the jungle. 'There's something moving out there.'

Lowery's throat went dry. 'Vargas?' he asked, hopefully.

'No. Moving too quickly for them. Come on, we've got to get away from here.'

'What about the distress signal?'

Cory thought for a moment. 'We'll take it with us. It doesn't weigh much. We'll launch it as soon as we get a chance.'

'Right.' Lowery hefted the cage. It wasn't light, but they could take turns in carrying it until they felt safe enough to launch it. 'Which way?'

Cory gestured to the north, then held up a warning hand. 'Watch out for vargas,' he warned, and then led the way across the clearing and into the jungle. They had barely slipped into the trees when Cory gestured for his companion to halt again. They stood for a second in the darkness and shadows and stared back.

From the far side of the clearing, two Daleks emerged, and moved gracefully towards the abandoned scout ship.

'Get down and don't make a sound!' Cory whispered urgently. Lowery didn't need a second warning.

Two further Daleks moved from the trees, and the four of them closed in on the ship. One of them moved close, and examined the open hatchway. 'The ship is empty,' it announced. 'The crew have gone.'

The patrol leader dismissed this. 'We will search for them. Destroy the ship.'

The four Daleks moved back slightly, and four guns came up. The Daleks switched to their most powerful settings for the weapons, and all cut loose at the same second. Briefly, night was turned to day as a fierce white light bathed the jungle. As Cory and Lowery shielded their eyes from the glare, they could see the ship starting to melt and dissolve. Designed to stand the terrific heat of re-entry, the ship still was unable to survive the tremendous energy outpouring from the Dalek guns.

Lowery had heard many stories of the Daleks, but even the legends had never hinted at such raw power from four small weapons. 'It's disintegrating,' he breathed in shock. 'Just falling apart . . .'

More practical, Cory grabbed his arm. 'Let's get out of here.'

Lowery needed no second urging to follow. He saw Cory moving off in the fading light, and grabbed the rocket framework to follow. As he did so, something stung his hand, Wincing in pain, he pulled it back, and stared, disbelieving, at his palm.

In the centre of it was a single varga thorn, still quivering.

Panicking, Lowery ripped the thorn out and flung it away. Feverishly recalling what he had seen of snake-bites, he started to suck at the small red wound, trying to get the poison out before it could affect him. Then he heard movement, and whipped his hand away from his mouth.

Cory's face reappeared. 'Come on, man, come on!' he urged. 'They'll be after us in a minute!'

Lowery managed to calm himself and nod. If Cory noticed the sweat and fear, he obviously took it as being reaction to the Daleks. As long as the agent didn't suspect the truth! Lowery knew that if Cory discovered about the thorn, he would be killed instantly. Cory was not the type of man to take unnecessary chances. Lowery had to keep it hidden, and pray that the thorn hadn't had time to infect him.

As he stumbled after Cory, though, he could feel his palm start to itch terribly . . .

* * *

The four Daleks stood beside the twisted, glowing metal that had been the enemy ship. There was now no way off this planet for the aliens. The patrol leader turned to the nearest Dalek. 'Report destruction of alien craft to control.'

'I obey.'

The patrol leader switched its vision enhancers on. The infra-red receptors began to register the faint heat-trail of two humans away from the ship. 'Advise that we will now seek out the crew. Alert all patrols.'

Following the pathway, all four Daleks began their hunt of Cory and Lowery.

Trantis glanced up as the representative from Gearon entered the conference room. This was the final member of the alliance, a somewhat faceless creature with an egg-shaped head. Gearon wore a thick visor, since he came from a world almost perpetually in darkness. Without a pause, he moved to stand behind the lectern bearing his name.

The semicircular table was now filled. Trantis looked about, his facial tendrils quivering as he did so. He could sense the vague thoughts of the other representatives of their vast galactic sectors. Like him, they were eager to begin this grand alliance, and start their conquest of the Galaxy. Beaus, from the Miron systems, was hardest to read: it was a tall creature, half-vegetable, half animal. It looked like an animated tree, possessing two burning eyes. Yet, it too yearned for the battles to come, and the gaining of new territory for its species to seed. Warrien was inscrutable in his cowled hood, his pressure suit containing the atmosphere that he needed to stay alive on this oxygen-rich world. Similarly suited was the representative from the planet Sentreal. His dark face was wreathed in the chlorine fumes that he breathed, and a small radio antenna on his head kept him in constant contact with his fellow beings still on their ship; the inhabitants of their world were a communal mind, and isolating one from contact with others of his species would kill him. Malpha, the last of the members, was tall and colourless. His suit and his skin were white, save for the thick, dark network of veins that created a patchwork of his face.

The seven lecterns for the representatives were grouped about the semicircular table, and each representative stood behind his or its own lectern. Before them was a large circular table, whose top was a scale model of the Solar System. The sun lay in the centre, pulsing with mock life, and scattered about it in representations of their orbit lay the various planets. Malpha had to admit that the room was certainly very impressive. The lighting focused on this map, and each representative's eyes were drawn irresistibly towards this new territory that lay in wait for them.

Beyond the table, the Black Dalek and three subordinates stood. As ever, they were completely inscrutable. They moved slightly as they waited with apparently inexhaustible patience.

The document that the delegates were signing arrived in front of Malpha. With a swirl of his stylus, he signed it, and passed it down to the closest Dalek. The Dalek moved the paper to position it in front of the Black Dalek, who scanned it.

'It is done,' it stated. 'The seven great powers of the outer galaxies are one.'

The delegates all smiled – at least, those who could did. The others expressed their appreciation in their own styles. Malpha, the final signatory, tapped his lectern, and all eyes turned on him.

'This is indeed a historic moment in the history of the Universe,' he stated, in somewhat pedantic tones. 'We seven from the outer galaxies, joining with a power from within the Solar System – and with the Daleks. We represent the greatest war force ever assembled! Conquest is assured!' He stepped from his lectern to the table before them all. With a gesture, he indicated a small red ball on its surface. 'Mars!' he exclaimed, then swept it from the surface. It clattered off into the darkness. 'Venus!' Another swing, and it went flying. 'Jupiter!' It followed suit. 'The lunar colonies!'

At this moment, the Black Dalek's arm shot out, resting on the small blue-green ball next in line. 'They will all fall before our might,' the Dalek grated. 'But the first of them will be the Earth!' Its arm shot forward, and the small globe of the Earth flew from the table and into the blackness beyond.

It was no good. Lowery rested on a small rock, staring in despair at his hand. It was burning badly now, and he knew that the varga poison had infected him. He was racked with small sobs, half-pain, half-fear, and he was sweating badly. His head ached, his mouth felt dry. Another paroxysm of agony shot through him, and he could feel the alienness within his body growing, striving to take him over. Shaking all over, he stared in horror at the back of his hand. Desperately, he pulled at his sleeve.

His hand and forearm were covered in thick, white hairs. He was turning into a varga!

Trying to blot out the sight and the knowledge, he pulled his sleeve down, and closed his eyes. He wanted to scream, to panic, to run, to kill himself – but he knew that he was no longer himself . . .

Unaware of the torment in Lowery, Cory slipped back into the clearing. 'There you are,' he said, relieved. 'I thought I'd lost you.'

Struggling heroically, Lowery managed to stumble to his feet. He tried to act as though nothing was wrong. 'Where . . . where have you been?' His voice sounded odd, thicker, but Cory didn't seem to notice.

Ignoring the question for a moment, Cory moved over to the rocket and its launch frame. 'We've got to get this capsule off – and fast,' he said. He began to straighten it up, and detached the recorder for the warning message. 'There's a city down there, a Dalek city. I got quite close. Close enough to hear an announcement that came through the loudspeaker system.'

His hand was a mass of flame now, but Lowery bit back the pain. 'What . . . what did you hear?' He could hear a pulsing in his own ears, the sound of some alien ocean pounding at the shores of his consciousness. He could feel himself starting to slide down a long tunnel, a tunnel of blackness and despair.

Unaware of this, Cory worked on. 'Our Galaxy is to be invaded,' he said over his shoulder. 'Destroyed.'

It was too much. The pilot could no longer hold on to his thoughts. He buried his head in his hands, no longer caring that his white fur and sharp thorns were visible if the agent glanced up. It hurt too much to think, and he let his mind go, feeling the relief of simple obliteration. His mouth moved, and softly, he muttered: 'Kill . . . kill . . .'

'What did you say, Lowery?' Cory asked, finishing his preparations with the rocket. It was all set to launch now, as soon as he loaded the message. Just another couple of minutes . . .

'Kill,' slurred Lowery, and then with more force: 'Kill!'

Suddenly aware of what had happened, Cory jumped to his feet, his gun in his hand. 'The varga . . .' he breathed.

Lowery's pain-racked face finally broke into a contented smile. His features were starting to vanish behind a fine down of white hair, and thorns were sprouting from his skin. 'Yes . . . yes, I'll be one of them soon. Kill . . . kill!'

Lowery went for his pistol, but Cory was faster. The gun spat death, and the half-varga stumbled, then collapsed on to the ground. Cory looked down at the still form. It was better this way for Lowery. His mind was already destroyed, and his body merely the host for a repugnant alien parasite. Compared with that, death was pleasant, a friend to be welcomed.

Enough sentiment! He had a task to finish, and he had to warn the Earth. He triggered the recorder that he still held in his left hand, and began to speak into it in a low, urgent voice. 'This is Marc Cory, Special Security Service, reporting from the planet Kembel. The Daleks are planning the complete destruction of the Galaxy, beginning with the planet Earth. Together with the powers of the outer galaxies, they are assembling a massive war fleet.' He continued to speak, detailing the message that he had heard in the city. It was imperative that Earth was warned about the

30

traitor who was set to betray them all, and to bring the forces of the Daleks right into the Solar System. He concluded: 'Whoever receives this message must relay the information immediately to SSS on Earth. It is vital that defence measures be put into operation at once. Message ends.' He clicked off the recorder.

He turned to place the recorder into the rocket, and froze.

Four Daleks stood, watching him.

Cory had a single moment to realize that, after all his efforts, he had failed. Then the Daleks fired. His body was bathed in their lethal radiations, and Cory crumpled, falling lifeless to the ground.

The patrol leader looked down at his body, and then across at the corpse of the half-varga. 'Our plans for the conquest of Earth are safe. Whatever information he may have discovered has died with him. Return to the city.'

'We obey!' In unison, the four Daleks spun about, and set off through the jungle that held no terrors for them. In the clearing, all was peaceful again.

By Cory's dead hand, the recorder with the vital information in it lay unnoticed.

4

The Nightmare Begins . . .

The Doctor brooded over the controls. His hawk-like face was set in a frown of concentration and worry. For once, his old ship seemed to be behaving. The time rotor moved smoothly up and down, the indicators showed that they were moving through both time and space. He had never really worried about his own progress through the Vortex – his keen love of discovery made every landing an experience to be grasped and enjoyed. This time, however, he could feel only apprehension.

Suppose the TARDIS landed in some prehistoric world? Or a dead planet, without inhabitants or even air? What if they landed scant decades away from the medical care that Steven needed? The Doctor was not certain that Steven could live through another flight through the Vortex. That wound was badly infected.

Drumming his fingers impatiently on the console, the Doctor searched for signs that their flight was coming to an end. If only he could be certain that there would be help for his young friend when the ship finally landed! But – where and when would that be?

This hell-hole planet was even worse by night, when you couldn't see what was out there – but you could hear things moving about. Kert Gantry lay back against the rock in the small clearing. With the section of cliff-face at his back, he felt slightly safer. At least he now didn't need eyes in the back of his head. He winced with pain as he shifted to try to gain a little more comfort on the stony ground. His left leg was a mass of pain, despite the pills he popped into his mouth from time to time. Gantry knew he shouldn't be taking so many, but they helped him to tolerate the broken leg. He glanced down at the crude splint, and the torn legging, brown with dried blood. Of all the stupid things to do, to catch his foot in the rocks and fall!

Gantry wiped the sweat from his grubby face. He was normally a handsome enough man when he could wash and shave, but after three days in this nightmare jungle he looked dreadful, and knew he must smell just as badly. Gantry looked over at his companion with a little envy. Bret Vyon had been with him all that time, and yet still looked fairly presentable. His uniform was still in one piece, its dark colouring providing a measure of camouflage in the night. Vyon needed a shave, but otherwise he was his normal tall, thin, clean self. If you could ignore the shadows under his eyes from the strain, that is.

'Five Zero Alpha to New Washington,' Vyon snapped urgently, triggering the microphone on the portable sub-space radio he was adjusting as he called. 'Come in, please. Five Zero Alpha to New Washington. Do you read me? Over?' His voice threatened to crack, a sign of the strain he was under. His only answer was a roar of static. 'New Washington, damn you, come in!' Again, he was greeted by a loud hiss. Slamming the microphone back into its holder, he turned in fury back to Gantry. 'Nothing,' he explained, unnecessarily. 'Not a peep! I swear, when I get back to Earth, I'm going to have the entire staff of Communications Central court-martialled!'

Gantry laughed without humour. 'What makes you think you're going to get back?' he asked. 'You know damn well we haven't got a hope.'

If Vyon accepted that, he had no intention of admitting it. 'We're not finished yet,' he said, quietly.

'Oh, come on!' Gantry was past self-delusion and hope now. 'Use your head. *They're* out there, looking for us right now. They're bound to find us, and when they do they'll simply blast us out of existence.'

'All right, all right,' Vyon agreed angrily. 'What happens to us is not important. But if they get to us before we can report, the whole Solar System is finished. There'll be nothing anyone can do to stop them.'

'I know.' Gantry sighed, and settled back. 'Try them again.'

Vyon turned back to the transmitter. 'This is Five Zero Alpha to New Washington. Come in New Washington . . .'

When Lizan had joined the Special Security Service, she had envisioned an exciting career on the boundaries of known space – perhaps working in an embassy on Draconia, or Alpha Centauri, or one of the many worlds that Earth now traded with. Or perhaps in charge of a section of agents on the exploration ships that still sought out new worlds and new races. As her training had progressed, she realized that she would not end up in any such exciting posts, and she lowered her goals considerably. Maybe she'd end up working as a bodyguard for some politician, or as a security guard at Los Angeles Interplanetary. Never in all her worse scenarios had she ever envisaged ending up where she was: section leader in Communications Central.

She wore a neat, lime-green uniform – as opposed to Security's black – with a Communications flash on each shoulder. It was easy to stay smart on this duty; there was little enough else to do. She and her second – Roald – simply took the routine calls from the various agents on missions, and then relayed anything interesting to the Director of Communications. At the moment, there were just over a hundred missions in progress, and they were averaging one call to the Centre every hour, since agents didn't report in daily. Every single call for the last three weeks had been routine and none lasted longer than it took to say 'All clear.'

Lizan had realized long ago that the only way to endure such tedium was to distract her mind. She and Roald were in the middle of another of their drawn-out tri-d chess matches. They didn't bother monitoring their panels, knowing that nothing ever needed their attention. The room that they were in was one of eight that radiated out from the Director's quarters, and the two walls of the wedge were lined with their communications boards and the Galactic chart. This showed the Galaxy, with Earth, its colonies and its allies marked in a pale, pulsing blue. The other, nearer galaxies of the Local Group were shown also – though 'near' was a very relative term; all lay millions of light years distant. Several of those galaxies showed a bright red light, winking in its ominous ruby lights, and almost as large as the blue portion of the map.

Dalek space.

Lizan and Roald, hunched over their complex boards, failed to notice that one of the blue lights right on the edge of the Galaxy was blinking brighter and faster than normal. Instead, Roald moved a piece on the board. 'Unicorn to level four,' he announced. 'Check.' He was pleased when Lizan frowned; it wasn't often he could surprise her nowadays with a move like that! 'Checkmate in three,' he announced. The light on the map had gone back to its pale form now, as he spun about. The far end of the room was taken up with a huge screen, at the moment dark. 'So, what's it to be? I want to see the Venus-Mars game, and you want to see your hero, Mavic Chen.'

'He's not my hero,' Lizan retorted. 'I just happen to admire him, that's all. He's one of the few politicians who's actually done more than he promised to do when he was elected Guardian.'

'I'll tell you what,' Roald suggested, his hands moving over his keyboard. 'If we tune into Channel 403, we'll get the news. That should satisfy both of us – you can see Chen, and I'll at least get the highlights of the match.'

Lizan considered this. Technically, they were not supposed to use the screens for private viewing, but no one was likely to catch them at it. Even if they were caught, they'd just be told off mildly. What else were they expected to do to pass the time? 'And what if they don't show Mavic Chen?' she asked.

'That's not very likely. The Guardian of the Solar System is going away on holiday.' He had all the information laid into his board, but being the junior here, he couldn't call it on to the screen. 'He'll no doubt say a few well-chosen words. Every well-chosen word will no doubt be transmitted.'

Lizan wanted to agree, but felt her job demanded a little more attention to the rules. 'And what about the routine calls?'

'You worry too much,' Roald answered. 'The next one's Five Zero Alpha, and it's not for another twenty minutes.' After a moment, he added: 'Well? What about 403?'

Giving in, Lizan called out to the computer: 'Bring up 403.' To Roald, she said: 'Five Zero Alpha? Was that the patrol out looking for Marc Cory?'

'Yes.' Roald grinned, to prove he'd been keeping up on the weekly briefing sessions. 'The agent who disappeared near the planet Kembel. Probably crashed, so they think. Lots of space junk in that system.'

The screen had come to life as the computer locked into the broadcast frequency selected. The news show was already under way, obviously. On the screen, news anchor Jim Grant's face smiled, and asked a question that was lost. The picture then cut across to the man he was interviewing, Mavic Chen.

Even the cynical Roald had to admit that Chen was impressive. The Guardian was over six feet tall when he stood. He was sitting now, so as not to dwarf Grant, and even at ease, the man possessed the coiled strength of a wild animal. His trim, muscular body was covered with a light-coloured tunic, which had a darker pattern woven across his chest. Chen's face showed signs of an oriental ancestry, but much mixed with other races. His white hair was close-cropped, and his beard gave him an air of dignity. His eyes were deep blue, almost hypnotic as he stared out of the screen. When he spoke, his voice betrayed no signs of age, and his tones were deep, clear and precise.

'The mineral agreements with the Draconian Empire proved to be a little more complicated than at first expected,' he finished, obviously closing a previous question.

Grant smiled at him and the home audience. 'And now that it's concluded so successfully, I'm certain that no one will begrudge you a little time off. What are you going to do on this trip?'

'That I am keeping a secret,' Chen announced. 'I hope to be able to get away from all interviewers.' Grant gave a polite laugh, to show that he was not insulted. Chen smiled slightly, to show that he hadn't really intended to give an insult. 'So I'm just going to climb aboard my *Spar* and drift about the Solar System.'

Roald whistled in envy. 'That's what I *call* a vacation! If I had to travel around in outer space, I'd take one of those 740s. Elegant, luxurious, plus the ultimate in technology.'

Lizan snorted, good-naturedly. 'It hasn't got the speed.'

'Speed,' Roald answered haughtily, 'isn't everything.' He was warming to his subject now; Lizan suspected he watched too many commercials. 'All the comforts you can imagine, almost silent engines – the yacht even has a small laboratory, in case anything goes wrong while it's out there in space. Food machines designed by French chefs . . .'

'And an advertising campaign aimed at billionaires,' she finished, with a laugh. 'You'll never be able to afford a *Spar*!'

'I can dream, can't I?'

Throughout this exchange, neither of them saw the little blue light on the chart begin to flash again, urgently. Their attention was firmly rooted elsewhere.

On the screen, the interview was clearly drawing to a close. 'Is there anything you'd like to say to the citizens at home before you depart?' Grant asked, knowing full well that no politician could resist an invitation like that. Chen didn't disappoint him.

Leaning forward, to gaze intently, yet caringly, at the viewers, the most powerful man in the Solar System began: 'It is my fervent hope that the Solar System may continue along this path of peace, this path that has been made possible by the signing of the Non-Aggression Pact of 3975. Now, in this year of AD 4000, we can feel justly proud of that Pact. May the past twenty-five years prove that they are the dawn of an everlasting peace that will spread throughout the Universe.' Now, Chen's intense, fiery voice calmed to sooth the viewers with gentle familiarity. 'Let us go forward together, secure in the knowledge that life ahead is built on the cornerstone of richer understanding between neighbours, not only of the past and of the present, but of the future. And may it be on this cornerstone – so finely laid – that our society will bring peace, progress and prosperity to each and every one of us.' Chen sat back, with a slight smile on his face.

What Grant thought of the inspiring little speech was unreadable through his firm, professional smile. 'Thank you, sir,' he said. 'I'm sure that our viewers throughout the system echo your thoughts.'

The picture changed, to one of those cute filler items that all news broadcasts feel compelled to include. Lizan turned her attention back to the game and to Roald. 'Even you must admit that he's an impressive man.'

'Oh, yes,' he agreed. 'It's nice to hear his speech . . . again.' All politicians ultimately said much the same sort of thing, he knew. Public faces, and all of that.

Lizan grinned in triumph, and moved her dragon. 'Checkmate!' she announced, firmly. Roald stared at the board in disgust, not having seen that move coming at all. Lizan gazed upwards, just as the blue message light winked back to normal. 'Was that a flash?' she asked.

'When!' Roald turned around, but the map was perfectly normal. 'There's nothing coming through. Nothing *ever* comes through.'

Lizan sounded uncertain. 'I thought I saw one.'

'You're imagining things.'

'Oh?' she asked, sharply. 'So now I'm imagining things?' It was going to be one of those days . . .

'I don't hear anything,' Vyon finally said.

'Oh?' Gantry snapped. 'So now I'm imagining things?' He held his rifle at the ready, the tubes glowing faintly in the darkness.

'I didn't say that,' Vyon replied, trying to calm down his partner. Gantry was an able man, but his injury and their three days of running in this jungle were telling on his

38

nerves. Privately, Vyon was certain that Gantry *was* imagining things.

'They're out there,' Gantry whispered, conspiratorially. 'I know it. They're getting closer.' His eyes darted about, trying to make out something in the gloom. He wiped his sleeve across his sweaty foreheard. Both men tensed to listen. Weird cries echoed about them, the normal feeding sounds of the nights of Kembel. Dragging noises . . . sounds like screaming monkeys . . . the ticking of insects . . . All as it had been for three long, sleepless nights.

Suddenly, it all stopped, and there was a terrible silence.

Vyon's eyes flicked towards his companion, who had gone rigid with fear and apprehension. Licking his lips. Gantry turned to face Vyon. Before the man could speak, Bret put a finger to his own lips, and softly drew his pistol. Tensely, they waited for long, agonizing seconds.

The crack of a branch being broken sounded like an explosion. Both men swivelled to face the direction it had come from.

'There!' Gantry gasped. 'There – you heard it!'

'I heard it,' Vyon agreed, softly. 'Come on. We're going to get out of here.' He looked down at Gantry, who made no effort to move. 'Well, come on.'

Swallowing what little moisture there was left in his mouth, Gantry shook his head. Puzzled, Vyon dropped to one knee beside him. 'Look,' he said, calmly, 'what's the matter with you? You know we can't fight those things. Our firepower won't even scratch them. Our only chance is to hide.' He started to reach out to offer Gantry his support in rising. Gantry batted down his hand.

'How can I move with this?' he asked, bitterly gesturing to his shattered leg. 'Have you got any other bright ideas? If I try to go stumbling through the darkness, I'll just run into one of those spiked plants. I nearly fell on one before.' He shuddered at the memory. Anything was better than that!

'We won't go far,' Vyon wheedled. 'We'll just keep moving. I'll make sure we avoid the varga plants.'

'No, I'll hit one!' Gantry was being consumed by his

39

terrors now, and he was shaking at the thought. 'We both know what happens then . . . that could be what happened to Cory, couldn't it? He tripped . . . pricked himself on a thorn . . . and then . . . then turned slowly into one of those varga plants.' He shuddered.

Vyon sighed. 'You're letting your imagination run riot again. Besides, we've not seen any varga plants that look like him. Perhaps *they* took him prisoner.'

Gantry laughed at the ludicrous thought. 'You know they don't take prisoners!'

'All the more reason for you to come with me, then,' Vyon finished logically. 'Come on.'

Gantry shook his head firmly. 'No! This is no time for phoney heroics. I'll just slow you down, and we'll both be killed. Without me, you've got a chance – not a good one, but a chance. Just stay alive until you get that message through.'

Vyon knew that his companion was correct, but he simply couldn't abandon Gantry. Instead of agreeing, he tried to put an arm around the man. 'I'm not going without you,' he said, firmly.

The other man shoved him violently away, then whipped up his rifle, holding it trained on Vyon. 'Keep your hands off me,' he said, savagely. 'Now get out. Go on, get out of here, or I swear I'll kill you now.'

Bret stood slowly up, looking down into Gantry's eyes. The agent had been tipped over the brink by all his pain, his terrors, his imaginings – and his brave decision to sacrifice his life. He was in a mood where he might very well shoot Vyon. Without a word, Bret walked over to the transmitter, and bent to sling it over his shoulder. Then, back to his partner, he walked towards the jungle.

'Bret.' Vyon turned, and Gantry gave a half-smile. 'Good luck.'

Vyon could find nothing to say; both of them knew that Gantry was going to die, buying a little time in the hope that Bret might get his message through to warn the Earth. Finally, Bret nodded, and drifted silently into the jungle.

Gantry let out a long sigh of pent-up breath. He was still

shaking from fear, and it had cost him all of his reserves to flash even that half-smile. He shuffled across to a small rock, and used it to steady his rifle on. He flicked his filthy hair from his eyes, and scanned the jungle in vain, waiting. 'All right,' he muttered to himself. 'I'm ready for you now. Come and get me.' The jungle stayed silent and still. Wildly, Gantry looked around. 'What are you waiting for?' he called, louder this time. 'I know you're out there!' Still there was no response. 'Come and get me!' he yelled at the top of his lungs.

Finally, one of the bushes trembled, showing that there was movement behind it. Gantry's finger tightened on the rifle's trigger, and he began to fire crazily into the bushes. After a moment, the gun stopped. Gantry swore, and glanced down at it. Empty . . .

Wiping his sweating palms on his good leg, he reached into a breast pocket, and with trembling fingers, he withdrew another clip for the rifle. It took him three attempts to discard the old one and fit the replacement, since he dared not take his eyes off the jungle for a second.

There was another sound of movement, this time from behind him. Slowly, he began to turn, as a shape emerged from the blackness. A half-scream managed to begin, deep in his throat, cut off as the Dalek fired at him. For a second, his body glowed and twitched, then fell lifeless across the rock and his useless rifle.

A second Dalek glided out from the bushes. It scanned the area, then switched to infra-red. Its eye-stick now picked up footprints leading away into the jungle. 'One man still lives,' the Dalek intoned to its companion. 'Find and destroy!'

'I obey!' The second Dalek slid into the jungle, following the faint but betraying heat trail after Bret Vyon.

The first Dalek swivelled its head, scanning the small clearing. Seeing nothing else of interest, it too moved off, but in the opposite direction. Once it had gone, the noises of the night began again, timidly at first, then more bravely. Eventually, almost an hour later, one of the hungrier animals ventured towards the corpse in the clearing, wondering if this alien creature would make good eating . . .

5

No Ordinary Ship

Bret Vyon fled through the night as fast as he dared. The bushes for the most part were innocuous, but if he should run into one of the varga plants and touch a thorn . . . he didn't like thinking of the plant's toxins invading his system and breaking down his body, recreating it as another varga plant. No wonder it had obsessed poor Gantry so! A terrible way to die.

He was going too fast in the poor light, and his foot caught in a far-flung root. Unable to stop, he crashed to the ground. The transmitter slung over his shoulder took the brunt of the fall, and he heard its delicate circuits and crystals shatter. In horror, all he could do for a moment was to stare at the broken casing. Then, desperately, he struggled into a seated position, and tried to get the radio working again. He tried long after it was obvious that the device was utterly broken. Finally he stopped, and flung the useless box deep into the jungle.

Now what? He had to get a warning back to Earth. He had to! The Solar System had to be warned what it would be facing very soon. But how could he do that? The only other radio that he knew of was deep within the Dalek complex on Kembel – and as good as he was, he knew he stood no chance at all of getting in there to use it. That left only the possibility of escape. Could there be some way off this world? His own ship was a twisted mass of wreckage in the jungle somewhere. The Daleks' orbital stations had fired on it, bringing it down. The pilot had died struggling with the controls, buying time for Bret and Gantry to eject. They had seen the ship explode seconds later.

That left Bret the option of trying the Dalek space-port.

The idea of his being able to sneak in there and make off with a Dalek ship was ludicrous. But it was that or nothing. He couldn't afford to do nothing.

His bitter thoughts were broken by the weirdest sound he had heard since arriving on this planet. It seemed to rise from nowhere, in a small clearing just off the path. A roaring sound, rising and falling, somehow mechanical . . . he dashed through the bushes, and stared. The clearing was empty.

As he watched, however, a light began to shine and spin, and below it a tall box materialized from thin air, gradually getting more and more solid. With a final thump, the noise stopped. The light on the box went out.

The TARDIS had arrived on Kembel.

The Doctor wondered where they were. His navigational instruments were in good shape, but he was unsure how to calibrate them. It had never seemed that worthwhile, since he enjoyed his peregrinations normally. Now all he could desperately hope was that this would be a technologically sophisticated world, for Steven's sake. The Doctor gripped his lapels, glad to be back in his regular attire again. How he hated dressing up in those silly period costumes! His frocked coat, trousers and string tie were much, much more practical.

Katarina entered the control room from Steven's quarters. She could see that the altar was not making any strange motions, and the noises had almost all stopped.

'Have we arrived in the Underworld now?' she asked.

'No, no, nothing like that, I certainly hope.' The Doctor reached out and flicked on the scanner. The screen came to life, but it was impossible to make anything out on it. 'It must be night,' he muttered to himself. To Katarina, he explained: 'We are on another world. The people here – if there are people! – will not be as you know them.'

'Can you find help here?' she asked, simply. Her mind was set on the one problem of curing Steven, and little could distract her.

'I don't know,' the Doctor answered, honestly. 'But I

must try. I want you to stay here, and look after Steven. I will be back as quickly as I can.'

Katarina nodded. 'I will tend to your priest, Doctor.'

'Splendid.' He beckoned her over, and smiled encouragingly as she timidly approached the console. 'Now, you know which switch to pull to close the doors, don't you?' He showed her the correct control.

'This stick will cause the doors to close,' she said, and was pleased when he nodded. 'I understand the magic.'

'Good. I want you to do that straightaway, after I leave. I have my key to let myself in.'

'Key?' she echoed, puzzled.

Of course! In her day, they would 'lock' the doors with a bar across the inside! He pulled his key from the string around his neck and showed it to her. 'This, my child. It will open the doors from the outside.'

Katarina looked from the tiny piece of metal the Doctor held to the huge doors. 'It must indeed be a mighty talisman – to move such large doors with so small a piece of metal.'

'Ah, quite.' The Doctor had had enough of explanations. Now was the time for action. 'Remember,' he admonished her, pointing to the switch, 'as soon as I am outside – close the doors!'

As Bret watched this strange apparition, the door opened, and a very eccentric-looking person stepped out. His clothing looked as if it had been bought from some costumer of historical video-dramas – checked trousers, long coat, silk scarf . . . what kind of clothing was that for such a hostile world as Kembal? The old man was twirling a key on the end of a chain, which he then tucked into his pocket.

Bret slipped silently through the jungle, following the path that the old man was taking. Whether by luck or by judgement, he was heading directly for the Dalek city. Could this man be a Dalek agent, reporting in? Then that weird box might be Bret's way off-planet. He should be able to overpower this senile old character without any problem . . .

The Doctor ground to a halt, peering through the dark

vegetation. In the distance, he could see lights. He took out his collapsible binoculars, and used them to scan the area. Several buildings could be made out with their assistance. 'Ah!' he muttered with satisfaction. 'A city.' He continued his scan, and soon realized that the city consisted of about a dozen tall buildings, clustered about what appeared to be a space-port of sorts. There were a couple of small ships there. Technology! 'Perhaps it's more of a town,' he added to himself. 'I wonder where we are?' Well, what did that matter? 'Perhaps I can get some help . . . Hmmm, seems a strange place to put a city, right in the middle of the jungle. As if they wanted to hide it from prying eyes . . .'

Further ruminations were cut off as something rammed hard against his spine. It felt uncomfortably like a gun. In the course of his travels, the Doctor had felt more than his share of guns pressed against his back.

'Keep absolutely still and make no noise,' a voice hissed.

'What do you want?' the Doctor demanded. It was most uncomfortable, not seeing the person he was speaking to.

'You'll answer questions, not ask them,' the voice answered. 'Quickly – that machine you arrived in – what is it?'

'That is my TARDIS. It can travel through time and space . . .'

'Space?' the voice questioned, eagerly. 'That's good enough for me. I'm taking it over, right now.'

That was too much for the Doctor to accept. Ignoring the gun in his back, he spun about to face his captor. For an old man, he managed this swiftly, swiftly enough to catch Bret by surprise. The Doctor was not over impressed by what he saw: a tall man, tired-looking, unshaven and unwashed for several days. The only thing preventing him from expressing his opinion was the obviously functional blaster clasped in the man's hand. 'You're taking over nothing, young man,' he snapped, angrily.

Bret was not interested. He waved the gun significantly.

'You don't understand,' the Doctor added. 'That is no ordinary ship.'

'That doesn't bother me,' Bret replied. 'I can handle most ships I've ever come across.'

'But I assure you . . .'

'Save your breath.' Bret reached out to pull down a section of a vine in a nearby tree. 'I'm taking it anyway. Sorry, but that's the way it is. Just be thankful that I didn't kill you.' Without warning, he suddenly pushed the Doctor hard. Caught off balance, the old man toppled. Bret was on him in an instant, and used the vine to truss him up. Despite his struggles, the Doctor was soon tightly tied and left against a tree. Almost as an afterthought, Bret reached into the Doctor's pocket and withdrew the TARDIS key. With a cheery wave, he set off, leaving the Doctor to try to free himself.

Katarina used a wet cloth to wipe Steven's head. His fever was increasing, as the poisons spread throughout his body. She had seen this happen many times, having grown up during the ten years of war with the Greeks. Soon enough, this young, handsome priest would die.

Steven's eyes flicked open, and he struggled to focus on the girl bending over him. 'Vicki?' he croaked.

'Rest,' Katarina told him, pushing gently to keep him supine. 'The Doctor will return very soon. He has gone to get help.'

'Help?' Steven was having trouble concentrating. 'Where are we?'

'Travelling through the Underworld.'

That made no sense at all to Steven, even in his fevered state. 'I don't understand,' he muttered, struggling to remember. 'Vicki . . . we left Vicki in Troy . . . you . . .' He managed to see her now. 'You helped me. Smoke . . . that Trojan, and his sword . . . did the Doctor bring you on board?' He struggled to sit up. 'Who are you?'

Again, she gently pushed him back, trying to soothe him. 'My name is Katarina. I was the handmaiden of the high priestess Cassandra. But you must rest now. The Doctor will bring help.' Steven opened his mouth again, but she pressed her hand over it. 'Don't ask any more questions.'

Steven sank back, too weak to argue and, in moments, he was dozing fitfully again.

There was the sound of the doors opening, and Katarina leapt to her feet. The Doctor, back already! She rushed into the control room, only to halt in the doorway as she saw the dishevelled figure that entered.

Bret was astounded as he entered the TARDIS. Instead of the small, one-man ship he had expected, he had stepped into a huge room. Computer panels lined the walls, alternating with inset discs in a regular and eye-pleasing pattern. There was some kind of mushroom-shaped control panel in the centre of the room, and a door leading – where? It was impossible to fit all of this into a small blue box in a forest on Kembal! What had he stumbled into?

As he stared about, a young girl appeared in the far doorway. She was pretty, and looked frightened. Her dress was low-cut, with a short skirt, showing a good deal of very appealing flesh. Was he hallucinating this?

'Did the Doctor send you?' she asked, timidly.

Dragging his attention from her legs, Bret nodded. 'That's right. The . . . old man sent me.'

'You must help Steven.'

How many more of them were there in this thing? No time to worry about that, now. If the old man got free, there could be trouble; the best thing to do was to seal off the doors. He crossed to the control panel, but could make nothing of it. None of the levers, dials, switches, buttons or gauges was labelled. 'Umm?' he asked. 'Of course I shall help . . . Steven. What's your name?'

'Katarina.'

'Right.' He had no idea what was going on, but he had to take a few chances. 'But first we must shut the doors. There are some dangerous life-forms on this world. The . . . old man said you know the switch.'

Eager to please, Katarina nodded. With great care, she pushed home the magic stick. Even though there was no connection between the stick and the doors, the two doors hummed closed. She felt very proud of her mastery of this minor spell.

Bret walked slowly about the console, shaking his head in amazement. 'I've never seen anything like this,' he muttered to himself. For the first time, he felt a twinge of anxiety over his plan. 'I'm not sure I can do it.' He glanced sharply up at Katarina. 'How do you work this thing?'

'Only the Doctor knows his temple,' Katarina answered.

'What?'

She gripped his arm, urgently. Her mind was still focused on one thing. 'You must help Steven!'

Impatiently, Bret shook her off, and returned to the controls, hesitating. Which one? 'Of course I'll help him,' he called over his shoulder. 'But it's imperative that we get back to Earth.'

Katarine frowned. Did this fool not know that the journey through the Underworld was only possible in one direction? 'We can't get back to Earth,' she said. 'We've left it.'

'Can't?' Bret was beginning to suspect that this girl was not as foolish as she seemed. Maybe she suspected something? 'Katarina, are you sure you don't know how to work this?'

'How could I know?' she replied, simply. 'It belongs to the Doctor.'

Bret returned to his study of the controls. None of them made any sense to him. 'The old man said this was no ordinary ship.' He shook his head in despair. 'He was right.'

At that moment, everything went black for him, and he pitched forward, unconscious.

Steven gripped the console to prevent himself from following. He let the Doctor's spare cane fall to the floor. Katarina gasped and hurried over to support him. 'Fake,' Steven managed to gasp. 'Doctor would never have given stranger TARDIS key. Would have returned with him.' The effort proved too much for him, and his knees buckled. Katarina didn't have the strength to support him, and he crashed to the TARDIS floor also.

Looking from one unconscious form to the other, Katarina didn't know what to do. Was this some strange form of test laid on her by the gods? What should she do? What *could* she do?

The Doctor had finally recalled a few of those tricks taught to him by that young escape artist . . . Harry Hoodoo, or something. The vine fell away from his arms, and he rubbed the circulation back into them. Then he stopped to recover his walking stick. As fast as he was able, he rushed back to the TARDIS. With a sigh of relief, he saw that it was still there. He had been afraid that the young man who had attacked him would do something stupid and make it dematerialize. 'Physical violence, eh?' he said to himself. 'You don't know what you've let yourself in for!' He hefted his stick, practising for the blow he'd give that vandal.

He chuckled as he saw the reason that the TARDIS was still there. 'And you've left the key in the door!' he crowed. The ship could not take off like that; the safety functions would never allow it. 'Well, well, well, that's the first of his mistakes. Very foolish, very foolish indeed.' He chuckled. 'If it's a matter of brain versus brawn, I have him outmatched from the start!' He had conveniently forgotten the fact that Bret had won their first encounter. He opened the door slightly before withdrawing his key and pocketing it – just in case the foolish youth had managed to engage the dematerialization programme.

The Doctor stepped into the control room, and Katarina breathed a sigh of relief. Now things would be straightened out!

When Bret came round, he had a splitting headache. He also found himself firmly gripped from the neck down in something. He carefully opened his eyes, and saw the old man, standing by the control panel, with the girl. A younger man was on the floor, with a pillow under his head, under a blanket that had been hastily thrown over him.

'I wonder if our captive has any connection with the city below?' the Doctor was musing. 'There are one or two questions I must have answered.' He glanced around, and saw that Bret was awake. The young man was struggling to frcc himself from what looked like an ordinary chair. Chuckling happily to himself, the Doctor walked over to gloat.

'It's a little invention of mine,' he explained, haughtily. 'I call it a magnetic chair. There are no locks or ropes, but it possesses a force-field strong enough to restrain a herd of elephants, so I wouldn't waste your energy trying to escape. You'll still be there until I direct otherwise.' Then, ignoring the captive agent, he turned back to Katarina, who was once again mopping Steven's brow. 'How is he, my dear?'

'He's feverish,' she answered, in worried tones.

'Yes,' the Doctor agreed, abstractedly. 'By the way, my dear, I've found a city.' When Katarina showed no evidence of applause, he added: 'Just as I was about to ascertain a way down, that young ruffian set upon me.'

Katarina was not to be side-tracked. 'Can you get help for Steven?'

'Yes, I think so.' He gestured towards the captive Bret. 'I shall have to cross-examine him when I get back. But don't worry – you're safe. Just don't have anything to do with him until I return. He's unable to move until I press that little switch on the back of the chair. He's quite harmless.' To illustrate his point, the Doctor went over and patted Bret on the shoulder. 'Quite comfortable, I hope, young man?' Bret glowered at him, and the Doctor chuckled happily to himself.

'I shall be back shortly,' he promised Katarina. 'As soon as I get help from the city.' Once again, he left the TARDIS and set out through the jungle – this time being a little more careful, and stopping to listen from time to time. He heard a sound in the sky, and looked up. A large ball of light was passing overhead and decelerating fast, obviously heading for the city he had seen earlier. Clearly, then, it was a busy place – just the sort of place to have a medic on call! Excellent!

The Black Dalek slid into the reception area of the space-port. This was a large room, one wall of which was glass and looked out across the level landing site to the jungle beyond. The other walls showed certain concessions to the weaker humanoid forms, with several couches placed carefully out of the Daleks' paths. Several other Daleks were in the room already, obviously to provide a welcome for the approaching ship. As the Black Dalek entered, one of the others crossed the room.

'Control reports rocket one eleven in landing circuit,' it stated. 'Touchdown will take place in three minutes.'

'Is all prepared?' the Black Dalek grated.

'Everything is in readiness.'

'Pass permission for rocket one eleven to land.'

'I obey.' The Dalek glided away to pass the order on to Control.

The Black Dalek was pleased; plans were advancing as they should. The report to be made to the Dalek Prime would be an acceptable one. In a few short days, the masterplan would be complete, and none of the other creatures of the Galaxy would be able to stand against the Daleks. The final few pieces of the plan were coming together. The approaching ship was one of the most crucial portions of the plan left . . .

Moments later, the field lit up as the ship came down. It was a sleek, dark ship, with much ornamentation – the affectations of wealth. It touched down, and the landing lights died, leaving only the inside lights for the sole passenger to disembark by.

The Doctor emerged from the jungle by the buildings of the space-port. Remembering only too well his run-in with the last person he had met on this planet, he had decided to play his hand very cautiously, and watch the inhabitants of the city for a moment or two before revealing himself. Keeping to the shadows, he managed to approach the huge glass-fronted building that was obviously the terminal. Inside, he could make out movement, so he edged towards the window, and peered cautiously within. Instantly, he stiffened and withdrew.

'Daleks!' he spat. Here – his greatest foes!

* * *

51

Bret had watched Katarina ministering to Steven for a while in silence, and finally could stand no more. 'What's the matter with him?' he asked, brusquely. Katarina looked up, but didn't reply. 'I said, what's the matter with him?'

'He's sick,' she finally answered, realizing that talking to him could not be breaking faith with the Doctor's instructions. 'The Doctor says that he has poisons in the blood.'

Bret nodded – the maximum movement he could manage under this invisible restraint. Infection of the blood, from that gash in the young man's side. Well, if it was a simple infection, he could help there. It never occurred to him not to want to aid the young man. He had nothing personally against these people, and he had appreciated that perhaps he had approached this whole matter rather unwisely. It was becoming painfully apparent that this strange trio of travellers were not agents of the Daleks. He should have tried to gain the Doctor's confidence, not steal his ship. Well, perhaps the error could be rectified if he helped out here. 'There are some tablets in the pouch of my belt,' he informed Katarina. 'Give him two of them.'

'I cannot do that,' Katarina replied. 'The Doctor has gone to get help.'

'He won't find any on this planet, believe me. So why not try the tablets?' Bret tried to give her his most winning smile, but he suspected that his looks were marred somewhat by three days' stubble and grime. 'I hate to see anyone die through stupidity,' he added.

The girl didn't seem to follow him. 'I do not understand you.'

'For heaven's sake, girl!' he exploded, annoyed at her obtuseness. 'Take the tablets and give them to him!'

Katarina could not see any evil in the man, despite the Doctor's own caution. He seemed to be perfectly genuine. What harm could there be in doing as he asked? Even if his medicines were poison, they could hardly be worse for Steven than allowing him to die of the wound he had suffered. 'All right,' she finally agreed.

'Now you're showing some sense!' Bret exclaimed. He watched her, smiling, as she moved slowly over to him. She reached hesitantly for his belt, and found the small compartment at the front of it with his supplies.

'Is this it?' she asked, nervously.

'Yes.' Seeing how frightened she was, he said softly, 'It's all right: I won't harm you. This chair of the Doctor's is everything he claimed. The tablets are in that tube.'

Katarina took a small metal vial from the belt, and held it out. There was some form of fastener on the top, which she managed to prise off. Two small white stone-like items slid into her palm. 'Are these . . . tablets?' she asked, in wonder.

'What do they look like?' Bret snapped. 'Take two and put them in his mouth. They dissolve quickly and take effect almost immediately. Katarina nodded, and moved off towards Steven. Under his breath, Bret muttered: 'I'm glad she's not nursing me!' She seemed to be a trifle lacking in brain power, to say the least! Louder, he encouraged her as she gave Steven the two pills: 'He'll be all right now. You can leave him alone.'

As she stood back, Katarina felt very nervous. Had she done the right thing? 'I have no doubt that the Doctor will be angry,' she said. 'I have disobeyed him.'

'Don't be silly,' Bret admonished. 'When Steven recovers, the Doctor will be pleased at what you did. I just hope the Doctor gets back here soon.' He didn't relish the idea of staying tied up with Katarina to look after him. She'd probably kill him by accident! And only the Doctor could get this strange ship moving again. He must get back to Earth and warn them!

The Doctor pressed himself further into the shadows, watching keenly as the Daleks moved to meet the new arrival. Whatever was happening here, it was clearly something of vital importance. If it was this urgent to the Daleks, then it was imperative that he should discover what they were doing – and thwart their megalomaniac little schemes!

Footsteps sounded over the floor as the final member of

the Dalek alliance walked to meet the waiting Daleks. The Black Dalek moved forward to speak to the new arrival.

'We welcome you as we welcome all allies of the Daleks.'

The ally bowed formally, then straightened with the hint of a smile on his lips. 'I am honoured to be here – and to be part of your plan to conquer the Earth and all of the planets of the Solar System!' Mavic Chen stepped forward and followed the Daleks into the main conference room.

6

The Day of Armageddon

The Doctor had no idea who the human ally of the Daleks
was, but he had heard enough to understand that it was
time for him to make a hasty retreat from the area. He
glanced around the corner, and then froze.

A small Dalek patrol force was gliding over the landing
area, in the full glare of the lights, towards the new arrival's
ship. The leader paused, and ordered: 'A full guard is to be
mounted over the human ship. Maximum security is to be
observed for the duration of the conference. All sections to
security alert.'

That was definitely his cue to leave! Quietly, the Doctor
moved back into the jungle. He moved slowly away from
the environs of the city, seeking to evade the Dalek motion
detectors. Once he felt that he had passed from their sight,
he hurried his pace.

As he half-ran, half-stumbled through the jungle, he
paused from time to time to get his bearings. Once, as he
did so, he noticed a slight gleam of light on metal from the
jungle floor. Curiously, he used his stick to brush aside the
bushes, and found two peculiar things.

The first was a human skeleton. It showed signs of having
been part of some animal's feast, and had probably been
there a few months. He had no way of knowing that he had
solved the mystery of Marc Cory's disappearance, the
reason why Bret Vyon was here on Kembel. The second
thing that he noticed was what had initially caught his eye
– a small cassette recorder. The metal case had rusted
slightly from being out in the elements, but a stray beam of
starlight had reflected from the case at just the right second.
Thoughtfully, the Doctor tried to play back the tape, but it

was obvious that the batteries – or whatever powered the device – were dead. He slipped it into his pocket; he could always examine it later, in the safety of the TARDIS – and returning to his ship was the most important task at hand.

There wasn't much of a path to follow, and he certainly wasn't as spry as he once had been. It took him the better part of thirty minutes to retrace his steps to where he had left his TARDIS. Finally, though, he broke through to the small clearing, to see the familiar lines of his ship in front of him.

Something wasn't quite right, though! He froze, scanning the scene, and realized what had subconsciously alerted him. The door was open slightly, and he distinctly recalled pulling it closed behind him. As he stood in the shadows and watched, the unmistakable form of a Dalek emerged from the TARDIS, and it was followed by two others.

'Steven . . . Katarina!' the Doctor whispered to himself. What had happened? Had the Daleks found a way into the ship somehow and killed his young friends?

The Daleks moved around the TARDIS, examining it minutely. Finally, one swung its eye-stick about. 'Inform base security that a further intruder craft has been located.'

'I obey.'

The first Dalek then switched to the general broadcast frequency used by the patrols. 'All security patrols will converge on this area,' it ordered. 'Priority alert. Intruders to be located and destroyed!'

The Doctor began to edge his way back into the jungle, eager to be away from this spot. As he moved, he heard the slightest sound behind him, but before he could turn, a hand had clamped across his mouth, and a second about his chest. The Doctor began to struggle, then all went black for him.

In the clearing, the Dalek patrol had noticed nothing. The second Dalek had finished its report to the city, and now said: 'I am receiving a message from the Supreme Dalek. Security operation Inferno to be put into operation at once.'

The patrol leader acknowledged this, then switched again

56

to the general frequency. 'All units: evacuate patrols to safe areas. Begin countdown to operation Inferno immediately.'

Mavic Chen stood in the Dalek conference room. He had unavoidably missed the preliminary session of the alliance, having been forced to lay a false trail from Earth, in case any of those prying reporters had attempted to follow him. Now, he leafed through the transcripts of that session. A door opened at the far end of the room, and a Dalek glided down the avenue of light towards him. Chen felt a prickle of irritation. This whole affair was getting a trifle melodramatic for his tastes. A huge conference room, badly lit to focus on the table, clearly designed to impress the peasants. Well, he was not impressed! The Dalek drew level with him, another wad of papers held in place on its arm. Chen took the papers with a curt nod, and the Dalek turned and reversed its path to the door. As it was about to leave, Zephon entered. The Dalek politely stood aside, allowing the black-clad figure to sweep imperiously towards the conference table.

Chen glanced up from the papers, with well-concealed irritation. Zephon was clad from head to foot in black, and all that could be seen of him were two eyes in the shadows of his hood.

'I am Zephon – master of the Fifth Galaxy!' the dark figure announced. He was clearly impressed with himself.

Chen smiled. 'Of course! I happened to meet you before, at the Intergalactic Conference at Andromeda.'

'I did not attend,' Zephon replied, haughtily. 'And now you know the reason. The Daleks held a separate conference at the same time. None of the delegates from the outer Galaxies went to yours.'

'Forgive me,' Chen answered, with an inner smile. 'It must have been another cloak I saw. One looks much like another – from the outside.'

'Quite,' Zephon agreed, coldly.

'I have heard much about you. Your people were once the greatest warriors in the Universe.'

'And will be again,' the alien replied. 'Our alliance with

57

the Daleks and the other outer worlds will make us invincible once more!'

'Yes, yes,' Chen agreed. This being was obviously craving power and conquest in the worst possible way – with naked greed. He tapped the papers he had been glancing through. 'I have been studying the reports of the first meeting. The plan appears magnificent. The Daleks have a unique talent for warfare.'

The eyes burned into Chen, and Zephon suddenly said: 'There is something I do not understand. You are a man of great power, the Guardian of your Solar System. Yet your planet will be the first to be destroyed when the battle begins.'

'Why the surprise?' Chen asked. 'As you say, I am the Guardian of the Solar System. But that is nothing more than a part – however influential – of one Galaxy. I have gazed upon a night sky bright with a thousand million stars . . .' His eyes took on a faraway look, as he lost himself in the memory of a vision. 'I have reached out my arms to embrace them to myself, and always they have slipped through my fingers. Now I can feel them drawing closer, through the power that this alliance affords me.' He trembled, as pleasurable anticipation filled him. Then his eyes focused once again on Zephon. 'Would *you* be satisfied with just a part of a Galaxy?'

'The Solar System is exceptional,' Zephon argued. 'In its power lies influence far outside its own sphere. Surely by joining with the forces determined to destroy that power, you must set yourself up as a supreme traitor?'

If Zephon was attempting to provoke Chen, he failed miserably. 'Traitor?' the human echoed, and then laughed. 'An archaic word for so advanced a . . . man as yourself.' Chen was enjoying baiting this arrogant and offensive creature. 'Considering the number of planets that have risen in revolt and attempted to depose you over the years, you can hardly claim to be a patriot yourself!'

'I do!' Zephon hissed, furiously. 'Those who struck against me are no more, and I control all of the Fifth Galaxy with a rod of iron!'

'True,' Chen acknowledged. 'But then you do not understand the conflicting powers within our Solar System.' He was abruptly tired of this conversation. 'Come, let us take some air. This is hardly the time or the place for so serious a discussion.' He took the arm of his fellow delegate, and together they walked towards the exit.

From out of the darkness, a lone Dalek slipped towards a second door. It hissed open, and the Dalek moved through. Waiting was the Dalek Supreme. 'Report,' it ordered.

'Earth creature Chen must be watched carefully,' the Dalek stated. 'His ambitions exceed his usefulness.'

The Black Dalek had expected nothing less. The lesser life-forms always felt themselves the superiors, and constantly schemed and plotted. 'When he has served his purpose he, like the others, will be eliminated. Only the Daleks are supreme. No power in the Universe will be able to stand in our way! We shall be supreme!!'

Steven felt his head was ready to burst as he struggled back to consciousness. He opened his eyes, and managed eventually to focus them. Everything seemed so dark, and there were strange noises. He felt about, and realized that he was on the ground somewhere, and it must still be night. What was happening? The last thing he could recall was the TARDIS. He had been in the TARDIS with . . . with the serving girl from Troy, that was it! But what had happened since then?

He had made a small groan, and instantly Katarina was by his side, helping him to sit up. 'What happened?' he asked her. 'Where are we?'

'The tablets I gave you made you better,' she said, checking the dressing on his wound. 'But you must still rest.'

Steven was looking about in amazement. Trees surrounded them on all sides! 'What are we doing out here in the jungle?'

'While you were asleep, the evil ones came.' Katarina thought hard. 'The other man called them . . . Daleks.'

'Daleks!' Steven exclaimed. When he had first met the Doctor, the Daleks had been hunting the time traveller to kill him. Was it possible that those most implacable of the Doctor's foes were after him again!

There was a faint groan from a bundle in the darkness close by. Abruptly, Steven realized that the 'bundle' was actually the Doctor himself, and that he was recovering from a blow to his head. The Doctor struggled awake, rubbing his scalp, and looked about himself in amazement.

'Steven! Katarina!' His smile of joy to see his companions alive and apparently well changed abruptly to one of annoyance. 'What are you both doing here?'

'The evil ones searched for us,' Katarina replied, 'but Bret helped us to escape them.'

The Doctor wasn't sure he understood what she was saying, but knew he'd better take it a step at a time. 'Yes, well, whoever this Bret is, he's quite right. The Daleks are evil beings.'

'Bret is the man you put in your magic chair.'

'What? That young ruffian!' the Doctor exclaimed. He was beginning to suspect who had hit him over the head.

'He helped us!' Katarine protested. 'He had magic tablets that have worked their miracles on Steven. His wound is healing.'

'And you released him!' the Doctor accused.

'Was I not right to do so?' she answered. 'When the evil ones came, he helped us to flee from your temple to safety.'

The Doctor sighed. 'Yes, well, he wasn't to know that you were all perfectly safe from the Daleks inside the TARDIS.' Nor, of course, was Katarina. There was really no use crying over spilt milk. His head felt better now, so he clambered to his feet and crossed to where Steven lay. 'How do you feel, young man?'

'I'll be all right in a minute, Doctor,' Steven replied. He was feeling much better, and his head had stopped orbiting some far star and returned to life on his shoulders. Someone – Steven suspected that it had been this mysterious Bret – had left him some regular clothing to put on. The Greek battle skirt was getting more than a trifle draughty in the night air! On the other hand, he didn't want to change while Katarina was about. He gestured to the Doctor, who caught on.

Taking Katarina by the arm, the Doctor led her away from Steven to allow the young man to get dressed. 'And what else did this – ah – Bret tell you?'

'He said that this is the year 4000. He himself is trying to get away from the evil ones. He gave Steven some white tablets, and they have made him well again.'

'Quite so, quite so.' The Doctor thought about their situation for a few minutes. As he considered their options, Steven hurried up, tucking his sweater into his trouser waist-band. 'Well, young man, you'd better pull yourself together,' the Doctor said firmly. 'There's work to do – and I think we'd best start by finding this Bret person. He seems to know something of what is happening about here, mmm?'

Bret was prone, peering from the safety of a clump of thick bushes down towards the TARDIS. The Daleks about the machine were extremely active, especially with the arrival of two Daleks, both equipped with larger weapon arms than normal. These did not seem to be the usual laser guns, but were connected to a pair of large canisters on the back of each Dalek.

One of these Daleks turned towards the patrol leader. 'Inferno containers are ready,' it reported. 'The other patrols are standing by.'

The leader grated: 'Ensure all other units have withdrawn from the jungle areas. Countdown to Inferno will begin at once!'

In the bushes, Bret decided that it was time to get back to the others. From the sound of it, things were about to start heating up in a very literal way . . .

Steven was walking slowly up and down, getting used to having his legs under himself again. The wound in his side was neatly covered and healing under his clothes. Aside from the constant throbbing, it only really pained him when he raised his arms. Whatever had been in Bret's pills had worked wonders for him. His headache was nearly gone now, and he felt almost ready to tackle the world.

'Just rest for a moment,' the Doctor advised him. 'You mustn't try to run before you can walk.' He shook his head, sadly. 'Though it may yet become essential that you do.'

There was a sudden noise, and they turned in alarm, only to relax when Bret slipped out of the jungle to join them. Katarina, especially, seemed pleased to see him.

Bret was happy to see that the Doctor and Steven were on their feet. 'Sorry I had to hit you back there,' he apologized to the Doctor. 'But I couldn't take any chances on your making a noise with all those Daleks about.'

'That's quite understandable,' the Doctor replied, then hefted his stick. 'Allow me to repay the favour!' He started to bring the stick down, but Bret wrenched it from his hands. The Doctor was furious. 'Let go of my stick, young man!'

'Doctor, please!' Bret pleaded. 'There are Daleks all around us!'

This brought the old man out of his feelings of aggression. 'Well?' he asked. 'What have you learned?'

'They're up to something. I'm not sure what, but they're evacuating all their units from the jungle.' Now that the Doctor had calmed down, Bret handed him back his stick.

'They're calling off the search for us?' Steven asked, incredulously.

'No, no, no, young man,' the Doctor replied. 'I know the Daleks better than that. They have obviously hit upon some way that makes it unnecessary for them to search for us. I think we'd be well advised to try to get out of the jungle.'

'Are you sure that's not what they want?' Steven asked. 'To drive us into the open?'

'Possibly, possibly,' the Doctor agreed. 'But what's the alternative?'

'I don't know,' Steven exclaimed. 'I just don't think we should act without thinking.'

'I *never* act without thinking!' the Doctor snapped.

'I agree with Steven,' Katarina added. 'I believe . . .'

This was too much for the Doctor – advice from this innocent child! 'Now, look here,' he snorted, about to launch into another of his tirades.

'QUIET!' Bret yelled – and got it.

The Doctor was astonished. No one treated him in so cavalier a fashion! 'I beg your pardon?'

'I said quiet,' Bret answered coldly.

'Now see here,' the Doctor began. 'I simply will not be . . .' His voice trailed off as he suddenly realized that Bret had drawn his pistol and was pointing it steadily at him. 'Ah. I see you have a very sound argument after all.'

Bret had had quite enough from this madcap trio, and it was high time he took command of the situation and restored some semblance of order. 'Now listen to me, all of you. I don't much care what happens to the three of you – or myself for that matter. The vital thing is to inform Earth security that the Daleks are planning something big, using this planet as their base. If I have to kill you all to get that message through, I will.'

'You have to do something more than that,' the Doctor added. 'If the Daleks are doing something drastic, then we have to stop them.'

'Then here is your choice. You work with me – or die now.' Bret made a small motion with his gun.

The Doctor cleared his throat. 'You put the matter most succinctly. I think I speak for all of us when I say – considering the alternative – we're with you.'

The patrols had withdrawn now from the jungle, leaving only the pair of Daleks with their heavier guns. On a signal from the city, these Daleks opened fire – quite literally. Each was fitted with a flame-thrower, fed from the canisters on their backs. The liquid spray ignited, and fell in a cascade of fire on to the dry growths of the jungle.

The trees ignited, trailing fire down their lengths to the undergrowth. In seconds, an inferno had begun, spreading and growing as it snatched at further trees and plants.

Flames leaped into the still night air, and the creatures of the jungle depths began a howling, screaming panic. Thick black smoke was rising, blotting out the stars.

The Black Dalek surveyed the scene from the city with satisfaction. The curtain of fire would be certain to drive the intruders from the jungle and into the waiting Dalek patrols.

7

The Face Of The Enemy

'We must try to get back to the TARDIS,' the Doctor said, firmly. 'The Daleks cannot penetrate my ship, and we can use it to get to a safer planet, where you can contact your superiors.'

Bret grimaced. 'Doctor, that is impossible: the Dalek patrols have used your . . . ship as the rendezvous point for their activities. Our only chance is to try to steal a spaceship and escape.'

'Is that all?' Steven asked, sarcastically. 'There'll be even more Daleks down by their city, surely?'

'Perhaps not,' the Doctor mused. 'There was a spaceship that landed not too long ago. While I was in the city, I could see that it was being refuelled, ready for another flight. If we could somehow seize that ship . . .'

Bret nodded. 'Quite right. I think the first thing to do is to take a look at it.'

Something had been intruding on Steven's mind for the past few minutes, and he finally realized what it was: wood smoke. He glanced back, and saw a red glow against the sky. 'Look!' he cried, pointing.

Even at this distance, there was no mistaking the meaning of the glow. 'A wall of fire,' Katarina exclaimed.

'They're trying to drive us out of the jungle like frightened animals,' Bret said.

'And no doubt they'll be waiting ahead of us, waiting to mow us down,' the Doctor added, a curious twinkle in his eye.

'Then we'd best get out of here,' Bret snapped, moving away from the flames. As Katarina and Steven moved to follow him, the Doctor held up his hand.

'No, no – I think we should go this way.' He gestured to the west, along the front of the flames.

'Are you crazy?' Bret exploded. 'That's the way to the Dalek city!'

'Of course,' the Doctor replied, rather smugly. 'That's the last place they'll expect us to go! Use your head, my boy – they won't have started a fire that could engulf their rocket fuel, now, will they? Ummm? On the other hand, they will be waiting for us if we flee in front of the flames. If we're nimble, we can nip across the path before the flames cut us off and make it to the city. And I expect that most of the Daleks normally on duty in the city will be positioned over there in front of the fire, waiting for us. It might even make our purloining of a ship considerably easier.'

A large smile broke across the agent's face. 'Yeah . . . good thinking, Doc.'

The Doctor smiled also, with affected modesty. 'As you come to know me, you'll find most of my suggestions bear the mark of genius.' Then, abruptly annoyed, he stabbed a finger into Bret's chest. 'And don't call me Doc!'

Mavic Chen stood in the reception lounge, looking out over the space-port. His magnificent *Spar* dominated the scene, and he felt a great deal of pride in it. As he watched, the umbilicals that had been used to refuel and reprovision the ship withdrew. It would shortly be time for him to return to the Earth and to act as though everything was fine – until the Daleks struck . . . The horizon was a dull ruby colour, as the flames spread through the jungle.

'The magnificence of flames,' he murmured. 'Primitive, but efficient.'

Zephon regarded the sight also, and snorted. 'You, too, would have used ultrasonics?'

'If I had nothing better.'

The Master of the Fifth Galaxy turned his gaze on to the Guardian of the Solar System. 'The meeting must start soon,' he observed. 'You appear so keen to be a model delegate one might think you were afraid of the Daleks.'

Chen sighed inwardly. How had this overbearing fool

ever become the tyrant of a whole galaxy? He had no sense of subtlety or refinement – or wariness. 'A dangerous statement,' he suggested, silkily. 'Remember where you are.'

Zephon snorted again. 'Is the Solar System so far behind they believe the Daleks need to eavesdrop?'

What a fool! *Naturally* the Daleks would be monitoring them! 'Of course, not,' Chen lied.

'The Daleks needed me,' Zephon boasted, striking at his chest. 'Without my help, they would never have got the co-operation of the Masters of Celation and Beaus. We are on equal terms!'

'Really?' Chen asked, in feigned wonder. 'Three galaxies for the price of one!'

'I do not understand you.'

That was quite painfully obvious! Abruptly, Chen wearied of mocking this idiot. 'Perhaps I'm one who knows my place?' he suggested. 'Are you coming in to take your seat?'

Stung by Chen's words, Zephon shook his head emphatically. 'They will not start the meeting without me,' he stated. 'I feel like waiting . . . *here.*'

How petty! Chen shrugged; let Zephon incur the annoyance of the Daleks. He himself would simply bide his time, until the moment was ripe . . .

Bret led the party swiftly through the trees, for once not too worried about the roving vargas – they, too, would be fleeing the flames for safety, as fast as their stumps could carry them. To their side as they ran there was the blaze, the smoke, the smell and the crackling sounds of the spreading fire. From time to time, trees would collapse, showering sparks and smoke into the air. Twice, the small party had to dive for cover to avoid Dalek patrols, but the fire was on their side; the Daleks would be unable to use their infra-red optics, as the fire would drown any tracks left by the fleeing party.

Eventually, they came to the edge of the jungle, where the space-port began. Abruptly, Bret ground to a halt, and stared at the waiting ship in astonishment.

67

There was no mistaking that huge, circular craft, the fins about the ship, and the array of antennae. Every line breathed luxury and refinement, and only one man Bret knew had a ship like that. 'I don't believe it,' he exclaimed.

'You know that ship?' the Doctor asked.

'Of course! It belongs to Mavic Chen, the Guardian of the Solar System!'

'Well, you should be able to fly it, then,' the Doctor observed.

Bret couldn't find the words. 'Yes, but . . .'

'That's the one we'll go for,' the Doctor informed Steven and Katarina. They nodded, and Steven started to inch forward to check the path.

'I can't believe it,' Bret muttered. 'It doesn't make sense.' The trouble was that there was a hollow pit in his stomach that told him, with agonizing clarity, that it *did* make sense – a terrible, dirty kind of sense.

'Stop complaining,' Steven hissed.

'But you don't understand,' Bret explained. 'He's the ultimate power in the Solar System. What's he doing here on Kembel, with the Daleks?'

'We'll worry about that later,' the Doctor suggested. 'Right now, you had better stick to thinking of a way to steal his ship.' The Doctor tiptoed forward to the end of the wall that they were hiding behind, and scanned the open space carefully.

Some twenty feet away, a figure in a dark cloak was staring at the line of fire on the horizon. The Doctor ducked back, quickly, but as he did so, his cane knocked against the metal wall.

Zephon was lost in his thoughts of conquest and pillage, barely aware of the flames in the sky. It would be grand to have more worlds to loot and to grind beneath his army's heel, and to – he wrenched his thoughts back to the present. Was that a sound he had heard? He looked down the wall of the building towards the jungle, but saw nothing. Probably just a technician or a Dalek. Still, thinking about Chen's words made him wonder if perhaps the Daleks were spying on him. He moved slowly towards the edge of the wall, intending to take a swift look round, just to check.

A pair of arms shot out and dragged him forwards, and then something hit his head hard, and he lost consciousness.

Steven pulled Zephon's body round the corner, as Bret reversed his pistol once again and replaced it in his holster. The Doctor peered down at the figure, an excited gleam in his eye. 'He must be one of the delegates from the outer galaxies,' he observed.

Well, he won't sound an alarm now,' Bret added. 'Let's see about getting out to the *Spar*.'

'Just a moment,' the Doctor said, holding his arm. 'Don't be so hasty, young man. This just might be our chance to discover what the Daleks' plans really are.'

'What do you mean?'

'Really, for an intelligence agent, you are remarkably stupid!' the Doctor snapped. 'What I am suggesting is that I adopt this creature's rather outlandish costume and try to penetrate the conference.'

All three of his companions stared at him in horror. Steven was the first to voice his thoughts. 'That's suicide, Doctor!'

'It's out of the question!' Bret added.

'It would be a dangerous endeavour indeed,' Katarina finished.

In his usual fashion, the Doctor ignored them all, and began to tug at the fastenings on Zephon's form-enveloping cloak. 'Listen to me, all of you,' he hissed. 'Do what you can to secure that rocket ship.' As an afterthought, he reached into his pocket and pulled out the cassette recorder he had discovered earlier, and handed it to Bret. 'Here, I found this. I don't know if it's relevant or not, but do look after it, umm?'

Bret glanced at it in surprise – an Earth scout-ship issued warning recorder! 'Where did you find this?'

'In the jungle, of course. Stop asking silly questions.' The cloak had finally come free of the alien, and the Doctor began to don it, noting with satisfaction that it was an almost perfect fit. 'Steven, fetch some of those creepers from the trees and tie this creature up.' He then turned to Bret. He was starting to like the young man's direct ways, if not his occasional lack of imagination; then again, not everyone could be up to his own intellectual standards, and he had to make do with whatever tools he had to hand. 'I want you to give me enough time to penetrate that meeting and find out what's going on. Then I shall head back and join you on the spaceship.'

'And how long will that take?'

'I'll leave that to your judgement.' The Doctor had finished fastening up the cloak, and even Bret had to admit that he did look a good deal like the alien that Steven was now trussing up. The black cloak fitted the Doctor well, covering him to the neck. The hood on the cloak should complete the disguise, once the Doctor drew it over his head. The Doctor tapped Bret's arm, and said, quietly: 'Of course, if you hear any kind of uproar, you'll have to go off without me.' Bret began to protest, but the old man held up a hand. 'Please, spare me all of that. It is more important for you to warn the Earth than to save me.'

'You're a very brave man,' the agent observed.

'Rubbish, my boy, rubbish,' the Doctor snapped, testily. 'I'm only doing what has to be done.'

Bret grinned. 'I like you better all the time, Doc.'

'Yes, and I'd like you better if you remembered to stop calling me Doc!'

The conference room was almost ready now. The Black Dalek scanned the room, and noticed with irritation that one of the delegates was not present. 'Where is the Master of Zephon?'

Chen smiled unctuously. 'He will be here,' he said. 'Eventually.'

As Chen had expected, the Dalek did not take this news too well. It spun its eye-stick towards a subordinate. 'Search for him!'

Watching the Dalek glide away on its task, Mavic Chen felt a deep satisfaction. Capital! The more trouble he could stir up between the Daleks and these ridiculous allies of theirs, the better. When everything was finished, there would be that much more left for him to grasp . . .

The Doctor watched his three young companions scurry towards the large starship on the launch pad, and nodded with satisfaction. Now it was time for him to make his move. He had managed to conceal his own unease about his foolish plan from the others, but he was not at all sure he was being very wise. Still, they had to know what the Daleks were planning, and this was their best chance. Pushing his fears down, the Doctor pulled the hood over his head, and started walking towards the doorway to the building.

The door hissed open, and a Dalek glided out. The eye-stick spun to examine him. The Doctor swallowed instinctively, and hoped that his disguise was as effective as he had believed. If the Dalek suspected his identity for a second, his life would be forfeit.

'Delegate of Zephon,' the Dalek grated, 'the meeting is about to begin.'

The Doctor waved his hand, and the Dalek spun about and led the way into the city. As he entered, the Doctor seized his chance to look around. The walls and floors were all constructed of metal, since the Daleks found this easiest to travel over. It also served to carry auxiliary power for their units, in that strange form of static electricity they had mastered centuries before on their home world of Skaro. These Daleks could move freely about without needing metal below them, thanks to solar panels about their mid-sections, but they still constructed their buildings of pure metal.

One large window faced out at the space-port, but there was no one in the room now who might see Bret, Steven and Katarina as they crossed the open space to the *Spar*. The Dalek led the Doctor into a short corridor, and from there into a large, dimly lit room. Some twenty feet away, a meeting table was illuminated. About one side was the Black Dalek and several of its minions.

The Black Dalek! This had to be important, then, for

the Black Dalek was second in the Dalek hierarchy, and rarely left the planet Skaro. Now, more than ever, the Doctor knew he had to discover what was happening here.

'You seem lost, representative Zephon,' said Mavic Chen. The Doctor recalled seeing him land in the *Spar*, and there was no doubt now of his identity. 'Here is your place, next to me.'

The Doctor didn't dare risk speaking, so he grunted in reply, and moved to the lectern that the traitor had pointed to. Glancing around, the Doctor recognized no more than two of the other species present. These were beings from the outer galactic groups indeed!

The Black Dalek had had enough of delays. 'Representatives,' it stated, 'I have important news. The manufacture of the Time Destructor has now been completed.'

By the sighs and excited looks on the face of the other delegates, the Doctor realized he was the only one who had no idea what a Time Destructor was. Still, it sounded ominous enough, and given the Dalek capacity for inventiveness when it came to mass destruction and murder, it was certainly a weapon to be reckoned with.

Clearly, the Dalek was pleased with the effect its words had had. 'It lacks only its Taranium core to activate it. Mavic Chen will speak.'

A born politician, Chen could never resist the chance for a speech. He took from his lectern a small wooden box, about ten inches long, and five on either side, and then stepped out towards the large map of the Solar System. 'As your most recent ally and the newest member to stand in this great universal council, I am delighted to be able to make so significant a contribution to our conquest of the Universe!' Chen held the box up for them all to see. 'I now present you with the core of the Time Destructor. A full emm of Taranium, the rarest mineral in the Universe! It has taken fifty Earth years to accumulate even this small amount.'

Trantis looked annoyed. 'If it has taken so long for the Solar System to produce it, why was not one of the outer Galaxies asked to provide it?'

72

What an imbecile! Chen smiled politely, though. 'As the Daleks know, Taranium can only be found on one of the dead planets of the Solar System.' The Doctor knew that there was much truth in this. The Daleks had spent almost a century gathering enough Taranium from their own empire to power a time machine that they had sent after him a short while back. With the aid of his companions, Ian, Barbara and Vicki, the Doctor had managed to capture and destroy that time machine, crippling the Dalek time researches. Now, however, it was apparent that they were using Chen to gain access to further supplies of Taranium.

'Without this,' Chen continued, 'the Time Destructor is useless! All the plans made here could not succeed. I, Mavic Chen, give you the core of the Time Destructor!' With these words, he opened the box, and slid from the casing the core itself – a mechanism of shining metal, lattices of crystal and a faint glow from the restrained power of the raw Taranium.

The Doctor felt a chill clear down to his soul as all of the Daleks turned their gaze towards the core. What evil plans did they have for that small device?

The pilot swung about in his chair at the controls of the *Spar*. This was a dream of a ship! He loved being here, in the heart of the craft. The computers augmented his own skills perfectly, making the craft a joy to fly. He hated having to stay even a short while on planets, and longed to be back in space again, dancing between the stars! Well, with the reprovisioning now complete, they could take off as soon as Mavic Chen returned from his mysterious meeting.

The engineer who had been checking the circuitry waved cheerfully as he left the room. A moment later, he backed in again, to the pilot's surprise. Then the reason for this odd move became quite apparent as Bret Vyon entered, and waved his pistol across the room. The pilot recognized the SSS uniform and stayed very still. He knew that agents were trained to shoot first and forget the niceties of life.

'Very sensible,' Bret approved. 'Now, come over here

73

and join your friend.' The pilot did as he was told, moving slowly and carefully, with his hands raised. Two more people – a young man and a pretty, bewildered-looking girl – entered the control room.

Steven whistled in appreciation. 'Hey, this is a bit of all right! Quite a lot different from the scouts I used to fly!'

'Really?' Bret asked, with interest. 'What sort of craft were they?'

Steven abruptly realized that this was the year AD 4000 – considerably after the period of time that he came from. 'Oh, it was before your time,' he said, quickly. To cover his mistake, he picked up a bale of wire and a pair of clippers. 'Right,' he ordered the two captives, 'turn round and hold your hands together.'

With a groan, Zephon finally woke again. His head hurt from the blow he had been struck, and he discovered that his arms and feet had been firmly tied. Obviously, there were still some of the intruders alive, and he had been attacked by them. Astonishment that they had dared to harm him was replaced by annoyance. He had to sound the alarm, and quickly!

The Daleks had instructed all the delegates where the various alarm points about the city were located. They believed in being cautious. Zephon knew that the nearest was just around the corner. He managed to struggle to a sitting position, and then pressed his back against the wall. Carefully, using his arms as best he could, he managed to push himself up against the wall, and eventually was standing.

Panting, he managed to jump a few inches forward. It would take a while, but he would be able to reach the alarm button, at least. Another jump, then another.

The tension in the conference room was electric now. Chen had placed the core down on the table, and it gleamed under the lights, drawing all eyes irresistibly towards it. Chen was enjoying the attention. 'I have one final question,' he purred, 'and I am certain that we will all be grateful if

74

the Supreme Dalek will answer it.' He paused for effect, and then asked: 'The date of the Earth's destruction?'

The Black Dalek looked directly at him. 'In Earth time,' it stated, 'one month from today.'

A broad smile of pleasure crossed Chen's features at this news. Soon, soon now . . .

Suddenly, the whole building was racked with an alarm klaxon sounding. Everyone jumped, and the Daleks began to spin about, seeking out what was wrong.

'Emergency! Emergency!' the Black Dalek called out. 'Intruder alert! All perimeter patrols report in!'

The Doctor knew that there could only be seconds now before his imposture was exposed. The delegates and the Daleks were heading towards the door leading to the space-port. Glancing around, the Doctor saw a second door on the far side of the room. With a swiftness that surprised even himself, he lunged for the Taranium core, and gripped it firmly. Then he ran for the second door.

The delegates were caught by surprise at this, and even the Daleks had not been expecting the move. Two of them spun about, but before they could fire, the Doctor was through the door, and jammed it shut behind him.

The alarms were still blaring, but at least this room was empty. If only there was a way through from here to the space-port! Otherwise he had simply delayed his execution.

As Steven and Katarina dumped the two bound and gagged captives out of the airlock, Bret settled down into the pilot's couch, and started to power up the *Spar*. He was vaguely familiar with the design, as all SSS agents were, but had never actually handled one of these beauties before. The controls responded to his slightest touch, and the engines caught and started their build-up in a second or two. He powered up the screens, the instruments, and began to get the feel of the controls. The ship hummed below him as the power built up steadily.

'Ready to lift when you are, Doctor,' he muttered to himself, priming the main thrusters.

Steven and Katarina returned, Steven rubbing his hands

together in satisfaction. 'They're out of the way of the blast,' he reported, 'and the rest of the ship is empty. You should see what they've got on this thing. I always did want to travel in style!'

'This craft is a ship?' Katarina asked, in awe. 'It is most beautiful, but I see neither sails nor oars. How then will it move?'

'Like a dream, believe me,' Bret informed her. It was a shame she was so stupid, because she was really rather a pretty thing. He couldn't understand why she seemed to be so out of things.

At that second, the alarms went off outside. The instruments picked them up perfectly within the ship, and the trio looked in horror at the screen.

'Something's gone wrong,' Bret snapped. 'We can't give him any longer.' On the scanners, he could see Daleks starting to emerge from the city complex. He reached for the main switches, only to be stopped by Steven.

'What are you doing?' Steven asked, shocked. 'We can't just leave the Doctor here!'

'He knew the risks he was taking,' Bret answered, pushing Steven aside. Steven jumped back.

'I won't let you!'

The time for rational discussion had passed. Steven knew many forms of fighting, but Bret was a trained agent. A single blow to Steven's stomach left the young man sprawled on the foor, gasping for breath.

Bret turned back to the controls, only to have Katarina hurl herself on to his arm. 'You cannot desert the Doctor! We must wait for him!'

Strangely reluctant to hit this innocent girl, Bret instead slammed his fist down on the thruster controls. 'The matter is academic, girl,' he snapped. 'We lift for space in fifteen seconds.'

Below them, they could feel the power of the *Spar*'s main engines building towards the peak required to take them into the sky.

8

Devil's Planet

A flashing light caught Bret's eye. 'The outer door!' he cried. Steven and Katarina had left it open when they had dumped out their captives. 'It must be shut! Quick, or we'll all be sucked out into space when we take off!'

Katarina wasn't certain what he meant by the words, but his sense of urgency needed no translation. The young Trojan ran after him back to the airlock door. Bret moved to hit a large, red button there, and then paused, a smile creasing his tired face.

'Doctor!'

The old man, puffing and panting, had arrived at the airlock at almost the same second. He held out a hand to be helped in. Bret took it, dragged him unceremoniously inside, and hit the button to close the door.

As he did, the engines built up to a terrific whine, and the floor beneath Katarina began to shake. She was thrown to the floor, and held in place by the terrific acceleration of the take-off. Not understanding, she was terrified.

'What is happening?' she called, looking frantically around, then staring in terror at the Doctor.

'It's all right, child,' he called, from his own position on the floor. 'Just a rather rough take-off. It seems to be this young man's usual manner of doing things. It will ease in a moment.'

'Sorry, Doc,' Bret apologized. 'We didn't have much time to waste, and when I heard the klaxons going . . .'

The pressure stopped, abruptly, and all three of them could sit up again. 'That's quite all right,' the Doctor replied. 'You acted correctly.' Bret stood, and helped the

Doctor to his feet. The old man stabbed his chest with his finger. 'But I shan't tell you again not to call me Doc!'

Steven appeared in the doorway to the control room, relief written all over his face. 'I thought I heard an argument, Doctor. It's good to see you made it.'

'Argument? Me?' The Doctor sniffed. 'I suppose I'd better check that the controls are set properly.' He strode past his companions, into the control room.

The Black Dalek entered the central control room on Kembal, and studied the floor below. The monitor supervisor raised its eye-stick.

'Attitude seven,' it reported. 'Speed three thousand. Rising.'

'Ship has attained gravitational escape velocity,' a second reported.

'Cut in automatic trackers,' the Black Dalek ordered.

The supervisor did so. 'Trackers operational.'

'Charge neutronic randomizer.'

From a further console, another Dalek reported: 'Ship is entering the range of the orbital stations. Weapons are ready.'

'Do not destroy!' the Black Dalek ordered, almost in panic. 'The core must not be destroyed!'

The Dalek acknowledged, and began shutting down the weapons systems of the satellite defences of Kembal. The fleeing aliens would have to be allowed through this barrier.

'Stand by randomizer,' the Black Dalek commanded. 'The intruders must be taken alive.'

Bret sat back from the controls, a smile of deep satisfaction on his face. 'That's it,' he reported. 'We're now locked in on a direct path back to Earth.'

'How can we return to Earth?' Katarina asked, puzzled. She pointed to one of the screens in front of him. It showed the hazy outline of Kembel. 'We have just left it.'

'That's not the Earth,' the Doctor explained, gently.

Bret had had quite enough of all of this. 'What's wrong

78

with this girl?' he demanded of the Doctor. 'She doesn't seem to know anything!'

Steven smiled. 'She's from Troy.'

'Troy!' Bret echoed. 'But Troy was destroyed thousands of years ago.'

'Quite right,' the Doctor agreed, not wanting to get into complicated explanations. 'That's why her knowledge is a trifle out of date. Yours, however, seems admirable on the matter of piloting this ship.' He had cast off Zephon's robes, and now took a comfortable chair. 'Now, I think it's time we took stock of our situation.'

Steven and Katarina followed his lead. Bret swung the pilot's chair around to face him. He looked at Katarina with wonder, but tore his attention back to the Doctor.

'What exactly do we know?' Steven asked.

'Only that the Daleks have allied themselves with the governments of the outer galaxies,' the Doctor began.

'And that they are planning an invasion of the Earth and the other planets in the Solar System,' Bret added.

'Well, at least we've not got a chance to warn Earth,' Steven observed. 'How long will it take us to get there?'

'Three days,' said Bret.

The Doctor rubbed his hands together, and chuckled with satisfaction. 'Excellent, excellent! I think it unlikely that the Daleks will be able to act before that time – particularly as I've got this!' Dramatically, he withdrew the core of the Time Destructor from the folds of his cloak.

Bret looked at the glowing instrument with puzzlement. 'What is it?'

'A small device that feeds from the energies of Taranium.'

'Taranium!'

Raising an eyebrow, the Doctor asked: 'You've heard of it?'

'That can only be found on the planet Uranus,' Bret exclaimed, taking a closer look at the device. 'It would take years to mine that amount.'

'Fifty years, to be precise.' Seeing the baffled expressions on the faces of Steven and Katarina, the Doctor deigned to explain. 'Taranium is probably the rarest mineral in the Universe. You have to process billions of tons of ore simply to get a milligram of it. It has the quality of being able to absorb enormous amounts of energy.'

'And if that energy is released,' Bret added, 'and harnessed . . . well, then you've got a pretty potent force at your command.'

Steven eyed the small core with respect. 'So what are the Daleks going to do with it?'

The Doctor shook his head, thoughtfully. 'I'm not certain. They have developed a weapon that they call a Time Destructor.'

'What's that?'

'I wasn't able to stay around and find out, my boy.' He stared at the Taranium core as if seeking inspiration. 'The Daleks have been studying time for almost a century, and they use the power of Taranium to effect their control of it. If you recall, when I first met you, the Daleks were hunting me down in a time machine – and that was powered by a small amount of Taranium – even less than is present in this core.' He looked seriously at his three companions. 'Whatever the Daleks wanted this for, it must be terribly dangerous – and terribly evil! But – it is unable to function without this.'

'And we've got it,' Bret said, happily, and sat back in his chair. 'Then I don't think we have to worry too greatly about the Dalek threat any more.'

'You're quite wrong, young man,' the Doctor said, vehemently. 'Dangerously wrong! Oh, certainly, we've got this . . .' He tapped the core carefully. 'And because we have it, the Daleks will go to any lengths to recover it.' Dawning awareness showed on the faces of the others, and the Doctor nodded grimly. 'We haven't escaped from danger – in fact, the danger has barely begun!'

The conference room had calmed down somewhat since the launch of the *Spar*. Unable to think of anything else to do, the delegates clustered about the table, muttering to themselves, and watching the Daleks' activities. Both Mavic

Chen and the furious, humiliated Zephon kept to themselves, though. Eventually, the door to the control centre hissed open, and the Black Dalek glided back into the room, followed by six others. They took their places about the table, and the delegates understood that they were expected to do likewise. As soon as everyone was standing at their lecterns, the Black Dalek scanned them all. Finally, it spoke.

'The core has been stolen by enemy agents. The council must determine who is at fault here.' The eye-stick rested firmly on Zephon. 'It was through your negligence that the intruders entered the conference.'

That was too much for Zephon's pride to bear. 'Had the Daleks made complete security arrangements,' he retorted hotly, 'then the intruders would never have reached the city!'

'Had the Master of the Fifth Galaxy been less arrogant,' Chen suggested, carefully, 'they would not have found a means of access so . . . conveniently waiting.' He laid a slight stress on the last words, implying that Zephon knew more than he was telling.

Zephon realized this, and scowled. 'I believe the intruders came from the Solar System,' he accused.

'Indeed!' Chen calmly raised an eyebrow. 'Did you see them?'

'No.'

'Then your allegation is preposterous.'

The silky, obsequious human was getting on Zephon's nerves. He pointed at the man, trembling in fury. 'How did the intruders know that the Taranium was here, and that it was to be handed over, if they were not from the Solar System?' Dramatically, he spread his arms to include the other members of the panel. 'None of the other representatives here knew what Mavic Chen was bringing.'

The Black Dalek's eye-stick moved to cover Chen. 'Explain,' it commanded.

Chen looked carefully about. 'This is ridiculous,' he said, finally. 'Why should I arrange for the mining of the mineral to be carried out in secret for fifty years only to have it stolen?'

'A thirst for power!' exclaimed Zephon, accusingly. 'Perhaps you wanted to use the core for yourself!'

'How?' Chen countered. 'Only the Daleks know how to assemble the Time Destructor. *I* only provided the vital ingredient.'

Zephon knew that the other delegates were becoming more and more convinced of Chen's innocence. He realized that the Black Dalek was looking at him again. 'I did not know about the core!' he cried. 'How could I?'

'You knew about the intruders,' the Dalek pointed out.

Looking about wildly, Zephon retorted: 'We all did! *You* were going to deal with them! You said . . .'

'Silence!' The Black Dalek had had enough of this foolish prattling. 'It is agreed that you are guilty of negligence.'

His influence now strangled, Zephon drew himself up to his full height. 'You cannot do without me,' he said, coldly. 'If I go, the Masters of Celation and Beaus go with me!'

'You threaten our unity?' the Black Dalek asked.

'I have nothing to say,' Zephon anwered, summoning all of his tattered pride about himself. 'I will leave now.' He cast one final stare of disgust at his fellow delegates about the table, and then turned his back on them.

The way to the space-port was blocked by four Daleks. For the first time, Zephon had a twinge of fear. His arrogance drained away, and he turned back to see six impassive faces and seven eye-sticks regarding him.

'Destroy him!' the Black Dalek ordered.

The four Daleks fired. Zephon screamed, twisted and fell, a smoking corpse. The other delegates carefully looked away from the body. The Black Dalek studied each one in turn, then spun to face the supervisor.

'Where is the ship now?'

'Course seven zero seven. It is approaching the influence of the planet Desperus.'

'Order the pursuit ships to positions,' the Black Dalek commanded. 'Prepare the randomizer.' It turned back to the delegates. As expected, they were trying to pretend that the death of Zephon had had no effect on their unity. 'The core will be recovered,' it promised. 'The intruders will be annihilated!'

The Doctor replaced the Taranium core in his pocket and smiled at Katarina, Steven and Bret. 'You young people are very fortunate,' he informed them. 'Very few people have ever seen this much Taranium.'

Steven wasn't all that impressed. 'Well, now that we've seen it, what do we do?'

'We do nothing,' the Doctor replied airily. 'And by doing nothing, we do everything. Do I make myself clear?'

'Not at all,' Steven said. The Doctor was hardest to deal with when he was feeling smug. 'What was all that supposed to mean?'

'My dear young man,' the Doctor smiled, 'you ask so many questions. Why not be like Katarina over there? She doesn't ask hundreds of questions – she simply looks and learns. Why don't you try the same thing?'

Katarina was seated by Bret at the controls. She stared at a small, milky-looking globe on the main screen. This business of pictures that moved was very strange to her. She reached out, and her fingers touched something smooth. 'What is this?' she asked.

Thinking she was referring to the planet, Bret looked up. 'Oh, that's the planet Desperus,' he explained. 'We have to pass close by it. It's called the Devil's Planet.'

'Anybody live there?' asked Steven, interestedly.

'Live?' Bret snorted. 'Exist would be a better word for it. Haven't you ever heard of that place?'

'We've – ah – been out of touch with things for a while,' the Doctor explained hastily, to stave off further questions. He knew that Bret would not believe the truth about the TARDIS.

'Oh.' Bret shrugged. 'Well, about fifty or sixty years ago, the crime rate was getting rather out of hand on Earth. Prisons became pretty full, and the towns were getting quite dangerous places to live. You risked your life walking alone in the streets.'

'The pleasures of civilization,' the Doctor interposed, caustically.

'Quite. Then Mavic Chen was elected as Guardian of the Solar System, promising sweeping reforms.' Bret considered what they now knew of Chen's motives. 'Anyhow, one of his ideas was borrowed from the primitive past. In the 20th century, one of the nations used to send its criminals to an island. Virtually no one ever escaped. And civilization was free of such men. Well, Chen used Desperus for something like that. Murderers, the criminally insane, those sorts of people, were all shipped here and left to fend for themselves. No wardens, no guards – and no escape.'

'Poor things,' the Doctor observed.

'Poor things nothing!' Bret retorted. 'They are all killers, kidnappers, and worse. They are thoroughly depraved, and unfit to live in the company of their fellow men.'

Katarina shuddered as she contemplated the globe on the screen. 'I am glad that we are going past that place of evil.'

'So am I,' Bret assured her, fervently. 'I doubt we'd live long down there.'

In the control room on Kembal, the Dalek technicians were all working at their panels. The large screen at the front of the room showed the path being taken by the stolen *Spar*. Its course was drawing closer to Desperus all the time.

'Ship is at closest approach,' the supervisor finally announced.

'Operate the randomizer!' the Black Dalek ordered.

There was a subdued hum from the controls, as the technicians obeyed. Outside, a bluish beam of light shot into space, travelling a very carefully calculated trajectory . . .

Bret stood over the course computer, matching figures with the calculations he had made earlier. Finally, he smiled up at the others. 'We're making very good time,' he announced. 'In fact . . .'

The *Spar* suddenly lurched, as its artificial gravity field

84

cut out, then returned and stabilized. The four of them looked towards the controls, to see a dull blue light dancing across the panels. Several banks of fuses exploded, showering the room with sparks.

Bret raced for the controls, closely followed by Steven and the Doctor. A quick test showed him that something had gone seriously wrong. 'There's no response,' he muttered, trying to get anything back on-line again. His fingers were burned slightly as he tapped at the computer keyboards. The whine of the engines had changed their pitch slightly, and the Doctor glanced at the scanners.

'We're changing course,' he announced, gesturing. Desperus was growing larger on the screens.

Nothing Bret was doing was having any effect on their flight. 'The steering thrusters won't fire. I can't get her back on to course!' Bret snapped open one of the computer banks. Smoke wafted out. He withdrew a plug-board, to reveal a charred mess. 'The control computers have been burnt out and overridden!'

'Can't you switch to manual control?' Steven asked.

'That's not feasible,' Bret snapped. 'I can't control all the functions of the ship at once – even if the panels were working.'

'We're picking up speed,' Steven observed, watching the few instruments that were still operational.

'Naturally, my boy,' the Doctor said softly. 'We are now under the influence of the planet Desperus. No doubt we are heading down there by the most direct route – and a rather abrupt halt when we hit the surface, I imagine.'

Bret swore, and slammed his fists down on the controls. 'And there's absolutely nothing we can do to stop the ship from crashing!'

The Dalek control room was a hive of activity. The supervisor looked up towards the Black Dalek. 'The ship's instrumentation is now randomized,' it reported.

'On course for the planet Desperus,' a technician added. 'Impact will occur in three units.'

'Engage remote control,' the Black Dalek said.

The technician obeyed. In front of it was a scaled-down panel similar to the one in the *Spar*. It tested the controls, and examined the computer readings. 'The ship is now under our control,' it reported.

'Reduce the descent velocity,' the Black Dalek ordered. 'The ship must be allowed to make a soft landing. The Taranium core must not be harmed.'

At that moment, Mavic Chen strode into the room. He noted the activity of the Daleks with mild amusement, and then crossed to where the Black Dalek was waiting. 'It looks as though you have them.'

The eye-stick focused on him. 'They are under Dalek control.'

'Excellent.' Chen looked around the room. 'Allow me to compliment you on the efficiency of your machinery.'

The Black Dalek did not like the patronizing tone that Chen had adopted. The human still had delusions that he was superior to the Daleks. 'Dalek technology is the most advanced in the Universe.'

'No doubt,' Chen agreed. 'Yet you still have not recovered the Taranium.'

'Dalek pursuit craft are on their way to Desperus. We shall recover the core shortly.'

'I'm delighted to hear it,' Chen smiled. 'Well, now that matter has been settled, I think I should head back to Earth. If the intruders were from there, I shall find out and prevent further trouble.'

The Black Dalek swung about. 'A special ship has been readied for you, and is at your disposal.'

'Thank you. I shall make all of the final preparations for the destruction of the Earth, and then return to join you here before the month is out.'

'All will be ready.'

'Good.' Chen turned to leave, and then spun around. 'We really don't want any more mistakes, do we?' He smiled pleasantly, and then strode from the room.

When the door had hissed shut behind him, the Black Dalek turned back to the main control floor. The arrogance of the human traitor was becoming harder to endure each moment. It would be a great moment when the usefulness of the specimen was finished – and the Guardian of the Solar System could be exterminated, along with the rest of the human race!

The violent pitching of the *Spar* was steadying now, as the four helpless passengers strapped themselves into the acceleration seats. The planet's edge filled the main screen, showing weathered landscapes, interspersed by patches of vegetation.

'We're slowing down!' Bret called, incredulously. 'I don't understand it!'

'I'm afraid that I do,' the Doctor said, coldly. 'Only too well. The Daleks have gained some form of remote control over this ship and are guiding us in for a landing. Never underestimate their ingenuity, young man – it could prove fatal!'

'Why don't they just let us crash?' asked Steven.

The Doctor gestured towards his pocket, indicating the bulge of the core. 'Because of this, dear boy. They daren't risk damaging it.'

'Then that obviously means one thing,' Bret said.

'Exactly!' the Doctor agreed. 'They will follow us down and come after us!'

9

Dangers In The Night

The cave was both dark and wet. A small fire in the centre of the space burned miserably away, as though it had long given up hopes of illuminating the place. Water dripped in the background. There was a smell of dead meat and unwashed bodies that pervaded the place. Three crude beds had been made from rushes from the swamps outside, but only one of these beds was occupied.

Kirksen sat in the centre of the cave, by the fire, smiling happily to himself. Kirksen was the only one of the three convicts who did smile, which always worried Bors and Garge, because Kirksen's smile was not sane. This time, however, Kirksen had a reason to be happy. He had made himself a knife.

It hadn't been easy, but Kirksen had spent a month on the task. He had found a small area in the hills where there was an outcropping of flint – though he had not informed his companions of this discovery. From half-recalled lessons of his youth, Kirksen had managed to chip away at the flint, bit by bit. After several failures, he had finally succeeded in re-inventing the stone knife. Now, using water and a stone, he was making certain that the blade of the knife was sharp. He had wrapped and tied grasses about the 'handle' to protect his hands, and the knife was finished.

He giggled softly to himself. Then he wiped his thin, unkempt hair from his eyes, and looked towards the one occupied bed. With his back to Kirksen lay Bors, sleeping.

Kirksen hated Bors as he had never hated anyone. Bors was the boss; he kicked Kirksen and Garge constantly into line, obeying his commands and whims. Kirksen was afraid of the crude strength of Bors, but with his knife, he now knew he could deal with the bully. Slowly, he crawled across the floor to the sleeping man, staying low, his knife raised and ready. Finally, he loomed over Bors, and brought the knife gently down until it almost touched Bors' neck.

In an explosion of movement, Bors came awake and grabbed the hand that held the knife. His raw strength started to bend the wrist. Pain shot through Kirksen's whole arm, and a knowledge of failure.

'I meant no harm,' he whined. 'I swear, I meant no harm!'

'I should kill you,' Bors snarled, twisting the arm again, and bringing tears to Kirksen's eyes. The old knife-wound on Bors' forehead, the relic of an earlier, failed attempt by some other man to kill him, throbbed in the uncertain light of the cave.

'No, Bors, no,' Kirksen whimpered. 'I wouldn't have harmed you. You know I wouldn't.'

Bors glared at him in disgust. 'Only because you're a weak, spineless cretin.' He looked at the flint knife. 'Give me that.' He twisted Kirksen's arm again, so that the man howled in pain.

'No, no – it's mine,' Kirksen wailed, like a child losing a favourite toy.

Bors paid no attention, but kept up the pressure on Kirksen's wrist. Finally, Kirksen was forced to release the knife, which clattered to the floor. With his other hand, Bors scooped up the knife. Then he flung the trembling Kirksen from him, rolled over and tried to get back to sleep.

Kirksen fell back, perilously close to the fire. Scrambling to his feet, he stood, panting and massaging his injured wrist. How he hated Bors! How he longed to kill the man! His eyes flickered about, finally coming to rest on a large stone that was used as a table. He glanced over at Bors, who contemptuously had his back to him. He could do it! He could kill Bors, now! Kirksen bent, gripped the rock, and lifted it up. A nice, heavy rock, and all it would take would be a single blow, to crack open Bors' skull . . .

There was a sound from the entrance. Kirksen hastily let the rock fall, and put his hands behind his back. Bors spun over, glaring at the cave entrance.

Garge ran in, his heavy stick now being used to support him, instead of as a weapon. He was a thickset thug, with a heavy beard, and was panting hard.

'What are you doing here?' Bors demanded. 'You're supposed to be on guard.'

'Rocket . . . coming . . . in,' Garge gasped, trying to get his breath back.

Bors snapped to his feet in one fluid motion. 'Prison ship?'

Shaking his head, Garge finally got his breath back. 'That's what I don't understand. It's a type I've not seen before. And it's nowhere near the landing zone.'

'Where will it touch down?'

'Hard to say, yet. But if it follows its present course, somewhere in the swamp.'

A cracked grin crossed Bors' face, showing his broken teeth. 'This could be what I've waited for all these years,' he laughed. 'A way off this stinking planet!'

Happy to be the bearer of good news, Garge also smiled. 'You think it's in trouble?'

'Why else would it be coming down? Nothing but the prison ships are allowed to land here. It must be in trouble.' He grinned again. 'Let's get out there and add to their troubles, shall we?'

He returned to his bed, and picked up a crude cudgel that lay there. Almost as an afterthought, he also picked up Kirksen's knife. Then he started for the entrance to the cave. Kirksen fell in beside him, hopping up and down, wringing his hands together.

'Bors – my knife. Can I have my knife back? I made it, and it's just right, and . . .'

Disgusted, Bors thrust the knife out to the little creep. 'Here. And this time, don't be afraid to use it.'

Almost slobbering his gratitude, Kirksen took the knife back reverently, and began to polish it with his worn-out sleeve. 'We going to kill the crew, Bors? We gonna kill them?'

'You think there's another way, maybe?' Bors growled. 'You think we could ask them nice, and they'll give us their ship?' He spat on the floor of the cave. 'You're a fool, Kirksen.'

Kirksen fell behind Bors, and stared at the big man's back, planning where he should stick the knife, when the time came. 'Don't worry,' he whispered, mostly to himself. 'I shan't be afraid to use it next time . . .'

The planet was every bit as bad as Bret Vyon had told them. The air was cold and dank. It smelled of death, and huge wings beat from time to time in the overcast sky. The *Spar* had come down in swampy ground, but this had luckily been firm enough at this point for the ship to land and sink only slightly. The Doctor surveyed the desolate landscape – rocks, lichens, and pools of smelly, stagnant water. He wafted his handkerchief across his nose again, and hurried back inside.

Bret and Steven had a good part of the main panel disassembled by now, and Bret was testing the various boards. Steven was over at the supply cabinet, and when Bret found a burnt-out component, Steven would search for the replacement as Bret called out the number.

'You're sure you have replacements for all of these parts, umm?' the Doctor asked Bret.

'Quite sure, Doctor. Government regulations are quite specific about carrying the parts, and this is an official ship. It'll be fully stocked.'

'The bureaucratic mind never changes,' Steven observed. 'How long will it take?'

Bret shrugged. 'A full replacement, about four or five hours. There's not the time for that, so I'm just replacing the major boards, and cutting out the sections the Daleks overrode. Shouldn't be too long.'

The Doctor snorted. 'Primitive fiddle-faddle and out-of-date machinery!'

'What are you talking about?' Bret asked in astonishment. 'This is the *Spar* – the most sophisticated ship in the history of space travel!'

'No doubt!' the Doctor sneered. 'And that's why we're stranded on this hell-hole of a planet!'

Steven couldn't take that criticism quietly. He had grown to admire this ship, which was far more sophisticated than the ones he had flown a few centuries earlier. Perhaps when compared with the TARDIS this ship *was* primitive, but . . . 'Oh, come on! The TARDIS isn't perfect. I mean, you can't even control where it's going.'

'Don't you criticize my TARDIS!' the Doctor yelled. 'For all you know of space travel – ah, you're still wet behind the ears!'

'Enough!' Bret called out. 'We have work to do, Doctor, so please don't distract us with pointless bickering.'

'Bickering!' the Doctor echoed. 'Young man, I *never* bicker!' Gathering his cape about him, he stormed out.

Bret glanced over at Steven. 'What's wrong with grandpa?'

'He gets like that from time to time. What's the next part you need?'

The Doctor was suddenly aware that Katarina was missing. Poor child, she must feel so useless here! She understood nothing of any of this. The Doctor was feeling a twinge of guilt over her predicament. It was never a good idea to take a travelling companion from a pre-technological world. They could never adjust to travel through space and time. Still, he had not been given much choice in the matter as far as Katarina was concerned. If she had stayed in Troy, she would certainly have died. And she had been helpful with Steven's wound.

He found her in the airlock, staring out into the dark night. Gently, he put an arm on her shoulder, and drew her under his cloak. 'You really should keep this door closed,' he said, quietly. 'You may catch a chill.'

She looked up at him, her eyes wide and trusting. 'You will look after me,' she said, simply. 'You are a good man – if, indeed, you are a man.'

'Yes, well, quite. I do try to be a good man. Ah, that is . . .' He waved his hand dismissively. 'Don't try flattery on me, child. I assure you I am quite immune.'

'I do not know where I am,' Katarina said, softly, gazing out into the night again. 'All my life, I have lived in Troy. This is all so strange to me. Yet, I know that I have not long to live.'

'What nonsense is this?' the Doctor demanded gruffly.

'It is not nonsense,' the handmaiden replied. 'When I served Cassandra, the prophetess, she told me that I should journey soon to my death, and that I should then achieve the Place of Perfection.' She smiled at him. 'This is a strange journey indeed, and must truly be the one that she spoke of. I shall be content when the time of my death arrives.'

Her utter conviction gave even the Doctor pause. Before he could think of a suitable reply, she gestured out into the night.

'There are lights out there,' she said. 'Torches!'

The Doctor glanced out. Far away, he could make out two – no, three – flickering lights. Obviously, their landing had not gone unnoticed! 'We had better inform Steven and Bret,' he suggested.

When they told their companions, Bret looked up, coldly. 'They're not coming because they're interested in our welfare.'

'How do you know that?' Steven asked.

'It's obvious, my boy, obvious,' the Doctor snapped. 'The men here have been abandoned to their wildest instincts, a warfare to stay alive. The landing of a ship, however badly damaged, offers them a possibility of escape.'

Nodding, Steven asked: 'Then you think there's a possibility we'll be attacked?'

'Possibility?' scoffed Bret. 'It's a certainty.'

'I'm inclined to agree,' the Doctor added. 'Are there any weapons on the ship?'

Bret tapped his holster. 'Just this.'

The Doctor pursed his lips and shook his head sadly.

'I'm afraid that will provide very little protection indeed against a large group of determined men.'

'It's all we've got.'

'Is it? I think not, dear boy. I think not.' The Doctor smiled, and tapped his head. 'We also have my brain, and we almost certainly have them outclassed there.' He gestured to the computer panels. 'You and Steven finish your work; Katarina and I will see about holding off the natives.'

He led Katarina back to the airlock, and thoughtfully studied the terrain. It was low and swampy, with trees interspersed in clumps. Fortunately for the ship, there were few rocks to have caused them damage on landing. The Doctor rubbed his nose thoughtfully, and then smiled. 'Well, my dear, what do you think?'

Katarina shook her head. 'All I see is swamp, Doctor – and those lights getting closer.'

'Swamp, yes, exactly.' Chuckling with glee, he rubbed his hands together and quoted: 'Water, water everywhere . . . which may be our solution!' He dashed back into the main part of the ship. Uncomprehending, Katarina took one last look outside, and then followed him.

The supervisor Dalek looked up at the Black Dalek from its panels and instruments. 'The exact location of the ship has been calculated.'

'Inform the pursuit fleet,' the Black Dalek ordered.

The supervisor moved to a monitor screen, which sprang to life at its touch. The picture showed the interior of a small Dalek pursuit craft, the single occupant wired into the controls. These ships were the fastest that the Daleks had constructed, and could outfly the *Spar* with ease. The squadron of eight ships was already approaching Desperus.

The fleet commander reported in: 'Estimated time of arrival, seven units.'

'When the Taranium core has been recovered,' the Black Dalek ordered, 'the fugitives are to be exterminated. Is that understood?'

'Acknowledged,' the commander agreed. 'We will recover the core, and then obliterate the fugitives.'

* * *

94

It was heavy going through the swamp. Bors, Garge and Kirksen – who was nervously bringing up the rear – all carried torches made from the dried swamp reeds. They burnt fitfully, and smokily, casting a pale glow over the water-logged ground. Every step squelched. The battered moccasins that the men wore were not up to this, and were leaking cold water.

Bors halted, then turned to the others. 'We're getting close now,' he said, gruffly. 'Put out your torches.' He plunged his own into the wet ground. It spluttered and died out. Garge did likewise, but Kirksen clutched his aloft, still nervous. 'Put your torch out,' Bors repeated.

'No,' Kirksen whimpered, staring about all over the sky. 'Please . . . the screamers . . . the only thing that scares them away is the light.'

Garge laughed. 'What are you scared of? They're only bats.'

'Bats?' Kirksen laughed, somewhat hysterically. 'Oh, yes – only bats! Vampires with six-foot wing-spans! I've seen them swarm all over a man and . . .' His voice broke off, and he started shaking.

Bors grabbed Kirksen's torch from the man and plunged it into the ground. It became very dark, and Bors could hear Kirksen's nervous breathing. 'Look,' he growled, 'if we keep together, they won't bother us.'

Garge was less sympathetic. 'Come on, will you?' he called. 'I doubt that we were the only ones who saw this ship land. We're lucky it was so close, but there'll be others after it soon.'

Bors nodded, which went unseen in the darkness. They could only just make each other out. Ahead of them, across the flat ground, was the ship. The lights from it were barely visible at this distance.

Kirksen whimpered to himself, looking upwards all the time. A sudden flurry of wings filled the air, and a dark shape blotted out the stars for a second. Throwing his hands over his head for whatever protection that might offer, Kirksen scuttled after his two companions.

* * *

The Doctor stood in the airlock of the ship, carefully stripping the insulation from one end of a heavy duty cable. Finally, he smiled in satisfaction, and checked his work backwards. The cable was wired into a switch by the door, by which Katarina stood, not understanding any of this.

'Now, my dear,' he said, slowly. 'When I call out to you, you know what you must do, don't you?'

She nodded. 'I must throw this . . . switch.' It made no sense to her, but the Doctor seemed all set to perform another feat of magic. 'What is it that you are doing?'

He chuckled happily to himself. 'I'm about to give our visitors a little shock,' he chortled. 'Yes, indeed, an – ah – electrifying experience.' His puns were never good to begin with, and these went completely over the head of poor Katarina. 'Now, you stay here, and I'll finish my little trap.'

He stepped down from the lock, on to whatever firm ground he could find. Anyone approaching the ship would have to come towards the main airlock, and the torches had been shining in the east. He walked a few yards out from the ship, and found what he needed. A long, fairly wide pool of shallow water blocked the approach from the east. Anyone coming towards the ship would have to pass through this.

There was a sound of wings beating in the air, and the Doctor became aware of something large above him. He spun round fast, shielding his face. Whatever the creature was, it was large, and aggressive. Slashing claws narrowly missed him as the creature gained height.

'Shoo!' he called, ineffectually. 'Get away, you nasty brute!'

It was obviously intending another pass. Carefully, the Doctor positioned his wire in the pool of water, and then dashed back towards the safety of the ship.

A moment later, Bors emerged from the gloom, and stared with grisly anticipation at the open airlock door. He hefted his cudgel, ready for action, and then looked back. Only Garge remained with him. 'Where's Kirksen?' Bors growled.

Garge looked around, astonished. 'He was right behind me a second ago.' He turned his head about, but saw no sign of the other man. 'Kirksen?' he called softly. 'Kirksen?' There was no reply, and Garge turned back to Bors. 'Shall I go and find him?'

Bors spat, disgustedly. 'No. He's probably fled back to the cave. He's scared stiff of the screamers.'

'Well, let him stay there,' Garge suggested. 'I feel safer with him out of the way. He's crazy, you know. I swear he is. One of these days, he'll snap and . . .' He made a suggestive sawing movement across his throat.

'OK,' Bors agreed. 'We should be enough for this. You know what to do.'

Together, they moved through the darkness. Bors had his cudgel at the ready, and Garge was hefting his long stick. Both were quite prepared to kill to achieve their aims.

As they moved forward, they knew that they would soon become visible to any look-out on the ship. At that point, they would have to rush forward and gain entry before the alarm could be sounded. They stepped periodically into the puddles of water that were scattered all over the landscape, and gave none of them a second thought.

In the airlock, the Doctor rubbed his hands together, as he saw the shapes moving towards the ship. Another few seconds and . . . 'Now!' he called to Katarina. The young Trojan threw home the switch.

There was a dull hiss of sparks, and the electrical charge flashed through the small pool of water in which both Bors and Garge stood. Both men cried, jerked spasmodically, and then collapsed. The Doctor patted Katarina, and nodded in satisfaction.

'That should be sufficient. I rather think my plan worked nicely.'

Bret poked his head into the airlock as the Doctor began to wind in the wire. 'Just about ready for take-off,' he said. Seeing what the Doctor was doing, he added: 'Electrical charge? There's not enough power in that to kill anyone.'

'Of course not,' the Doctor agreed. 'But there was quite

sufficient to knock them unconscious. You'd better learn now that I have no desire to kill anyone.'

It made no difference to Bret whether the convicts lived or died. He shrugged, and returned to the control room. The Doctor finished coiling the wire tidily away, and disconnected it from the electrical supply. He then followed Bret. Katarina took one last look out of the airlock, then followed.

For a few moments, the landscape was peaceful. Then, wheeling from the sky came one of the screamers. Flapping its huge wings, it hovered for a moment over the two unconscious bodies. Finally, deciding that this was no trap, it settled on to the nearer man, and began to feed. The scent of fresh blood attracted others in the vicinity, and soon Garge and Bors were lost under a cloud of feasting screamers.

They had escaped in the only way they ever would from this planet.

Inside the ship, Katarina, the Doctor, and Steven took their seats. Bret started to power up the engines, and smiled in satisfaction as everything came on-line. In moments, the power had built back up again, and they could all feel the ship straining to rise back into space.

'What's that red light?' the Doctor asked, gesturing to the panel at Bret's right hand.

'Mmm? Oh, the outer airlock door must have been left open.'

'I'll get it,' Steven volunteered.

'No need.' Bret pressed one of the controls, and the light went out. 'I managed to find the right panel when we were doing the repairs,' he explained. Then he smiled, somewhat nervously, and shot the thruster controls home.

The *Spar* rose, slowly at first, and then faster, up from the planet. The acceleration pressed them all back into their chairs, and they all watched on the screens as Desperus dropped away below them.

'Look!' the Doctor called out, gleefully, gesturing to the picture. 'The Dalek ships have made their landing! We couldn't have picked a better time to leave!'

They could all see the small shapes of the Dalek pursuit craft, all on the ground. Their Dalek pilots had moved out, and had been working their way towards the spot where the *Spar* had lain. Now the Daleks would have to return to their ships before they could follow.

'We've lost them now,' Steven grinned.

'Lost?' The Doctor shook his head. 'I shouldn't count on that, young man. The Daleks won't give up yet. They'll pursue us as close to the Earth as they dare.'

Bret was stabilizing the ship now that they were back in space. He began powering down the take-off systems and to cut in the main drive, ready to take up their path back to the Earth. Everyone's eyes were on him, so none of them noticed that the inner airlock door was opening slowly. A pair of eyes scanned the room, then settled on the back of Katarina's neck.

Kirksen raised his flint knife, ready . . .

10

The Sacrifice

Kirksen had not – as Bors had believed – returned to the
cave when he slipped into the darkness. Instead, he had
been hiding out close by his two companions. He had heard
Garge call, and ignored it, and then watched them move on
to attack the ship. Kirksen giggled to himself in the
darkness; he had it all figured out. Bors and Garge would
attack the ship. The crew would fight back. Even if his
companions won the fight, they would both be tired, and
perhaps one might be dead. If they lost the fight, then the
surviving crew would be tired. Either way, Kirksen could
jump the survivors, fresh for the fight. He'd make his
escape from this hell-hole of a planet, but he'd do it alone.

Then he had seen Bors and Garge electrified. Kirksen
fought down his panic, watching as the strangers in the ship
recovered their trap. When all was clear, he had started
edging towards the ship. The sudden descent of the screamers to feast off his former allies sent him scuttling quickly
for the only hiding-place left him – the open airlock of the
ship. He had tumbled inside, quivering, seconds before
Bret had sealed it for the take-off.

Once the ship had left Desperus's atmosphere, Kirksen
knew that he had almost made it to safety. He peeked
through the glass panel set in the inner airlock, and studied
the crew in the control room. There was an old man, and
two younger ones, working the controls. One of them had
a gun, but it was holstered. He could be a problem. Then
there was a young girl, standing with her back to him,
watching the control screens. It was perfect . . . exactly
what he needed.

Quietly, he opened the airlock door a crack, just far

enough to allow him to slip out silently. No one suspected that he was there until he grabbed Katarina's hair roughly, jerking back her head and laying his stone knife across her jugular vein.

At her startled scream, the three men whipped around. Steven started to move, but Kirksen shook his head. 'Back,' he warned. 'Stay back.' He giggled softly, his face contorting as he did so. 'Any of you come near me, and I'll kill her. You understand?'

Katarina struggled, trying to get free, but Kirksen kept his grip on her long hair, which he twisted cruelly. The knife constantly threatened to break her skin. Furious at this, Steven made a bid to step forward, but the Doctor restrained his headstrong friend.

'Careful, my boy!' he warned. 'I do believe he means what he says!'

'Oh, yeah,' Kirksen agreed, grinning. 'Yeah, I sure do mean it.' He pulled on Katarina's hair again, and giggled when she gasped in pain. 'Now – which of you is piloting this ship?'

'I am.' Bret's voice was cold and emotionless.

'Good, good. Now, you'll do *exactly* what I tell you to do.' He giggled happily to himself. 'You may be the pilot, but from here on, I'm the captain. Now, where are we headed?'

'New Washington, Earth.'

'No!' Kirksen screamed. 'Change it! We've got to go somewhere else!'

'We can't do that,' the Doctor replied, in alarm. 'It's vital that we get back to Earth! We must warn them of the Dalek power-base on Kembel!'

Kirksen shook his head, laughing. 'Oh, no! You're crazy. How long d'you think I'd stay free if we went back to Earth? They'd pick me up inside a week, and I'd be sent back to that filthy Devil's Planet!' He thought for a second. 'Change the course to Kembel.'

'Kembel!' Bret exploded. 'We can't do that! The Daleks are there.'

That didn't interest Kirksen directly. He had never

stayed in school longer than he was forced to, and knew nothing of history. 'That's right. Whoever these Daleks are, they'll help me. If they're against Earth, I'm on their side.'

'I very much doubt that the Daleks would see it quite like that,' the Doctor warned. 'They're evil creatures, thoroughly despicable!'

'Yeah? Well, I've spent twenty years with people like that. I'll feel right at home there. Set the controls!' He looked at the three men with fury. None of them moved. 'Set the controls!' he screamed again, this time making a motion across Katarina's throat with the knife.

Reluctantly, Bret moved to do as he was told. As he crossed past Steven, the younger man used his chance to snatch up a heavy spanner and throw it towards Kirksen. Only the convict's finely tuned reactions saved his head from being hit, and the spanner clattered off the wall behind him.

The Doctor, Bret and Steven all tried to move at once while Kirksen was off balance. Keeping his grip on Katarina, though, Kirksen lunged backwards into the airlock. Once he had Katarina inside, he slammed the airlock door control, and the heavy bulkhead hissed closed behind them.

Steven drew up short, then turned to Bret. 'You said you'd figured out the controls now – get this open from the panel!'

'No!' the Doctor cried, urgently. 'He could kill her in there before we could get near him.'

'But we've got to do something,' Bret protested. 'We can't just leave them in there. Poor Katarina must be terrified.'

The Doctor knew that she must indeed be frightened, but this was not the time for action. He only hoped that he could convince his two companions of that. Young men tended to be so impetuous! 'We have no alternative. At the moment, he is holding all of the high cards.'

Steven glared at the door, seeing Kirksen inside, holding the knife on Katarina. 'Look, he's got to be bluffing! He daren't kill her. What would he gain?'

'Normally, I would agree with you, my boy,' said the Doctor, slowly. 'But did you see his face? He's not sane, not sane at all. The normal rules of logic mean nothing when dealing with a mind like that. If we prod him too far, he might very well kill her.'

Bret nodded. 'Murder would be nothing novel to an inmate of Desperus.' He shook his head. 'We'll simply have to sweat this one out.'

The Black Dalek was not at all pleased with what had happened. Its eye-stick centred on the screen connecting the Kembel control centre with the Dalek pursuit fleet. The pursuit task force had allowed the intruders to escape with the core from Desperus. 'Estimated time of interception?' it demanded.

'Seventeen units.'

The Black Dalek ran the figure through its internal computers, and arrived at a decision. 'This would place you too close to the Earth. We cannot chance the humans becoming suspicious of Dalek manoeuvres so close to the Solar System. Break off pursuit and return to Kembel.'

'I obey.' The pursuit leader cut the communication beam.

Turning to the monitor supervisor, the Black Dalek grated: 'Contact Mavic Chen. He must recapture the Taranium core and the creatures who stole it.'

'I obey.'

As the supervisor turned to begin signalling Chen on their tight-beam channel, the Black Dalek spun about to face the mission controller. 'Destroy pursuit ships,' it commanded. 'They have failed in their mission. We do not tolerate failure.'

The controller moved to its panel, and keyed in a sequence. The long-range radar screens suddenly went blank. The Black Dalek glided out of the room. It was always a good incentive to the workers to show them the results of failure. It inspired them to work well and avoid making foolish mistakes.

★ ★ ★

Seeing that the three men were showing no signs of trying to prise him out of the airlock, Kirksen relaxed slightly. He loosened his grip on Katarina, and she managed to tear herself free from him. There wasn't far she could go, but she collapsed in a corner, hugging herself, and trying to stay brave. Kirksen saw her efforts, and then giggled. He moved slowly towards her.

'Pretty hair,' he whispered, still giggling. He reached out to touch it. Katarina shuddered. Kirksen ran his fingers through the locks, enjoying the feel of a woman's hair again. It was so long since he had felt anything this delicate. 'Pretty hair,' he repeated, then slashed down with the knife. Katarina squealed, but all he severed was a lock of her hair. Still giggling to himself, he began to wrap the hair in and out of his fingers. After a moment, he dragged himself back from his private world of madness and threw the hair aside. Then he crossed to the microphone on the wall and triggered it. 'Listen to me, out there,' he called.

The Doctor, Bret and Steven ceased their talking, and glanced towards him. Kirksen continued: 'Listen carefully. You'll do exactly as I say. *Exactly*.' Satisfied that he had their attention, he carried on with his thoughts. 'I'm not going to kill the girl. No, no, killing her – that would be silly. Then I wouldn't have a hostage.' He grinned again, his lop-sided, evil smile. 'But life could become very painful for her. I'm sure you know what I mean.' He raised the knife, so that they certainly would understand him. 'Unless you do exactly as I say.'

The Doctor and Steven, their faces mirroring the pain and fear for Katarina that they felt, moved closer to the airlock. Bret, on the contrary, moved towards the control panel. Seeing the Doctor and Steven peering in at him, Kirksen smiled again, then twisted, swiftly, and severed another lock of hair from Katarina's head. Holding up his hand, he turned his palm over, allowing the hair to fall gently to the floor. It was an unsubtle demonstration, but it provoked the fear that he wanted them to feel. 'Change course for Kembel,' he ordered. 'Now!'

Steven moved over to join Bret at the controls. 'There must be something we can do.'

Bret looked up, impassively. 'There's nothing.'

Wildly, Steven suggested: 'Why not depressurize the airlock?'

The Doctor snorted. 'That wouldn't work – they'd both be dead before we could get in there.'

'All right.' Steven thought hard. 'How about putting on space suits and going round the outside of the ship to the airlock. Then Bret could open the outer door . . .'

'And they'd both be shot out into space by the outrushing air!' the Doctor finished. 'It's quite out of the question.'

'Well, what *can* we do then?'

Shaking his head, the Doctor said softly: 'We'll have to do as he says. We'd better change course. Let him go to Kembel – and see if he likes his reception by the Daleks!'

'And what about us?' Steven asked. 'The Daleks might be glad to see us with their core, but they won't let us live.'

'I'll think of something,' the Doctor snapped, testily. 'Until then, we have no option but to do as he says.' He reached towards the controls.

'Get away from there,' Bret said, coldly, holding up his pistol. 'Go on, move away.'

The Doctor stared at him and the gun incredulously. 'What are you doing? That's a madman in there – we have no choice but to do as he says.'

'You may have no choice, Doctor,' Bret informed him, 'but I do. The important thing is to get to Earth and warn them about the Daleks.'

Steven couldn't believe it. He pointed wildly to the airlock. 'You want that maniac to use that knife on Katarina?' he cried. 'We have to change course.'

'I'm sorry.' Bret truly was sorry; he had come to like these three travellers very much. But when it was a case of their lives or his mission, he had no option. He tried to make them understand. 'The whole of the Solar System is in danger. I can't afford to let the life of one person jeopardize the lives of billions of people. I'm sorry.'

Steven was stricken. 'I don't care about billions of

people,' he said. 'They're just figures. Statistics. I care about that girl in there. She risked her life to save mine. I can't just abandon her.'

'We're going to Earth,' Bret said, flatly. 'If either of you tries to change that, I'll be forced to kill you.'

Kirksen was not a patient person. He was getting more and more annoyed as the discussion between the three men was being played out. 'They're not doing anything,' he told himself in disgust. 'They're not changing course.' It was obvious that they simply didn't believe he would do what he had said. He crossed to the microphone again, and slapped it on. 'You don't believe me!' he howled. 'I'll show you I mean it! I'll show you!' He moved towards Katarina, his knife at the ready. Perhaps he'd just cut up that pretty face a little, let her scream a lot . . . that would show them. Yes, that would do it!

'Please!' the old man called. 'We must have time! It's not a simple decision we face. If we don't go to the Earth, billions of people will die.'

'I don't care about people,' Kirksen snarled. 'I only care about me. And if you care about this girl, you'd better do as I say.'

Katarina swallowed hard, and summoned all of her courage. She did not understand everything that was happening. This travel between the stars was beyond her comprehension, for one thing. Yet she was not a fool. She knew that Bret, the Doctor and Steven had to get to Earth to warn everyone about the evil ones on Kembal, and what they were planning. She knew that while she was being held hostage by this madman, they were forced to consider doing as he demanded. She was the crux of the problem now. It all rested in her hands.

She suddenly knew what she must do. All her fear fell from her as she made her decision. Cassandra had been correct when she had prophesied her journeys. Now she would be correct about her fate. Katarina remembered how worried Bret had been about the airlock door being open when they had taken off from Kembal, and she had observed the Doctor operating the magic controls when they were on Desperus.

Before Kirksen could move closer, she jumped to her feet and brought her hand down hard on the outer door control.

Kirksen had time only to start a scream of sheer terror. The airlock door hissed open into the star-speckled darkness. The air shot both of them from the small chamber, sending them tumbling into infinity . . .

Steven stood, trembling, at the inner airlock door, his face contorted by horror. After a heart-wrenching second, he turned anguished eyes on the Doctor. 'She . . . she hit the wrong button.'

'I don't think so.' The Doctor was having trouble seeing straight. Uncharacteristically, there were tears in his eyes. 'She did what she wanted to.'

Bret, his gun away again, touched Steven gently on the shoulder. 'It must have been quick.'

The Doctor stared at the stars visible in the gaping lock. 'I hope she's reached her Place of Perfection,' he breathed, mostly to himself.

'Not that way!' Steven was having a great deal of trouble handling her death. 'Not like that!'

'She wanted it that way,' the Doctor said, firmly, getting control of himself. 'She wanted to save our lives. And, perhaps, the lives of all the beings in the Solar System. She deserves her perfection. That is the way I shall always remember her: as one of the daughters of the gods!'

Steven nodded, trying to accept what the Doctor was saying. 'A daughter of the gods,' he repeated, dully. The hard ache within him was not comforted yet. But perhaps, one day, it would be.

Trantis was fuming. It had been two days now since the intruders had fled the planet Kembel, and nothing seemed to have been done. The Daleks were certainly active, but none of them had deigned to inform the delegates of progress. It was as though they were considered unimportant. They had complained about this a number of times to one another, but none of them had had the courage to ask the Daleks what was happening. Trantis didn't lack the courage, but he felt that having to elicit information was beneath his status.

By the end of the second day, however, he realized that he'd either have to swallow his pride or remain in the dark. He eventually stormed into the Dalek control room, and looked around. When he spotted the Black Dalek, he marched over.

'What is happening about the Taranium core?' he demanded.

The Black Dalek spun around. Its first instinct was to order the alien from the control room, but that might cause problems. For the moment, the delegates were necessary. Finally, it replied: 'The ship is now approaching the Earth.'

'Then they have escaped?'

'No. Guardian Mavic Chen has been given his instructions.'

'To do what?' Trantis demanded.

The Black Dalek turned away, dismissively. 'It is not necessary for you to know.'

This hurt Trantis in his most vulnerable spot – his pride. He walked around the Black Dalek until it was looking at him again. 'As representative of the largest of the outer galaxies, I have the right to know!'

The eye-stick focused on him again. 'You will be informed as to what you have the right to know.'

Changing his tack slightly, Trantis said: 'We're supposed to be allies. You trust Mavic Chen – why will you not trust me?'

'We trust no one,' the Dalek replied. 'Particularly Mavic Chen.'

Trantis was interested at this piece of news. He wondered if Mavic Chen knew that. Chen had an over-inflated opinion of his own worth. It needed cutting down to size.

'Ship has entered Earth approach,' the monitor Dalek called out.

The Black Dalek ignored Trantis again. 'Inform Mavic Chen. This time, the intruders must be intercepted. The Taranium core must be recovered and the thieves must be exterminated. Exterminated!'

11

The Traitors

The *Spar*'s instruments were already registering their path through the Solar System. The Doctor hovered over Bret, as he threaded their way through the Solar defences. He was feeding out the correct recognition codes that would allow them to penetrate into Earth's orbit. Steven was still off alone, mourning Katarina's death.

'We'll be ready to land soon,' the Doctor said, in anticipation. 'We should have quite a reception.'

'That's what worries me,' Bret admitted.

Chuckling, the Doctor squeezed his shoulder. 'You'll soon get used to such gatherings. I have.'

'That's not what I mean,' the agent answered. 'We can't land at the space-port itself.'

'Oh?'

'Mavic Chen has had plenty of time to reach Earth before us, thanks to that enforced stop-over on Desperus,' Bret explained. 'It's possible that he's waiting for us. The landing field is where he'd expect us to come down.'

This had not occurred to the Doctor, who had been so happy they had made it this far unchallenged. 'Hmm, yes, I see. Well, where can we land, um?'

Bret called the information up on the screen. 'Just here,' he said, gesturing to the map. 'It's an experimental plant a little way outside New Washington itself. I've a friend there with connections who I think will help us.'

'Splendid.' The Doctor nodded in approval. 'I see you have it all well thought out, young man. I couldn't have done better myself. Well, carry on, carry on.'

Sighing to himself, Bret began preparing for the impending entry into the Earth's atmosphere.

* * *

Mavic Chen felt happiest back behind his desk again. It was the one place where he was in total control. Behind him was the huge map of the known Universe that the Science Section had had specially made for him. In front of him, his desk, with the built-in terminals. Quick movements of his fingers over the keyboards could bring him information from any place on the Earth – and from many places beyond it. In seconds, he could evaluate any situation and deal with it. This desk was the centre of his power, and the kernel of his sphere of influence.

At the moment, a piece of paper lay on the desk, the only thing marring its smooth perfection. On the other side of the desk stood Karlton, the head of Special Security Service, and Chen's deputy. 'So this is our traitor?' Chen said, softly, studying the paper again. It showed a picture of Bret Vyon, together with a brief description of him.

'That's him.' Karlton was dressed in the standard black of the SSS. His craggy features were lined with care, and his hair was thick and grey. 'Bret Vyon. One of the top men in the department. Born on Mars, Colony 16. He's a very able man. He and his partner, Kert Gantry, were investigating a missing agent, Marc Cory.'

'I don't need their life-stories,' Chen said. 'Merely their apprehension. And, of course, their deaths.'

'All agents have strict orders to shoot if they attempt to resist arrest.' A slight smile played over Karlton's face. 'I can't imagine Vyon not resisting arrest.'

'Vyon and Gantry never reported in from Kembel,' Chen mused. 'They must be the men who stole my *Spar*. They may, however, be working in association with some other creatures.' He considered the matter for a moment. 'I want all Special Security agents recalled to Earth. If Vyon and his accomplices are not captured within an hour, I want all of Central City cordoned off until they are found.' Chen stared off at the ceiling. 'Really, Karlton, I'm most disappointed with you. Allowing two security teams to investigate Kembel when you *know* how important it is that the place should remain untouched.'

Karlton replied stiffly: 'I've already given instructions

111

that *all* future operations are to be cleared with me before they are begun.'

Chen turned cold eyes on to him. 'If you'd done that in the first place,' he said, smoothly, 'we wouldn't be in this spot.'

Karlton didn't like the sound of that. 'Cory's mission was one he undertook himself,' he protested. 'It was done without official sanction at any time. He was like that. Then, when he vanished, I had no option but to send in an investigation team.'

'With Vyon?' Chen held up the wanted poster. 'One of your best operatives? Who would find out the truth if anyone did?'

'He was the closest,' Karlton said, sulkily. 'I had no logical reason to by-pass him. Besides, I thought that the Daleks would kill him for sure!'

'You must do better than that,' Chen said, standing. 'I would hate to have to lose you.' He stared pointedly at his deputy, and enjoyed watching Karlton squirm. Both of them knew that any such loss would end with Karlton in a grave.

The *Spar* entered the Earth's atmosphere rather unsteadily. The shuddering and buffeting the ship was receiving made itself felt inside. Steven grabbed hold of one of the panels to steady himself.

'Don't tell me we're going to crash?' he called. He could recognize a bad landing when he felt one.

'At this stage,' Bret snapped, impatiently, 'I may not be able to help it. My repairs on Desperus were rather makeshift, and some of the systems have failed. I'm having enough trouble trying to kill our speed.'

'As long as you don't kill us as well.'

Bret cast him a filthy look, then busied himself with the controls. Either way, it was going to be a close landing. If he was lucky as well as skilful, they should be able to walk away from it. What was it they always told you at the Academy? Any landing you walk away from is a good one? Well, they needed a good one now . . .

112

The ground came up at them fast. Bret struggled with the sluggish controls, forcing the ship to inch its nose up, and trying to lose some more of their forward speed. The wind outside was buffeting them strongly, and it was getting harder and harder to retain control.

The screens showed the plant below them, as Bret struggled to keep the ship in the air a few seconds longer. The buildings whipped past under them, and suddenly there was the meadow Bret had recalled. Crossing all fingers – at least mentally – Bret brought the *Spar* back down to Earth.

The ship hit hard, spun, and slid. Huge furrows were gouged in the turf, and the heat of the impact sent flickering flames along the grass. Finally, the ship lost its forward momentum completely, and it came to rest in the smoking soil, tipped over slightly.

There was no sign of life aboard it.

Chen had almost forgotten that Karlton was still with him as he stared up at the huge map of the Universe behind his desk. Stars, galactic clusters, quasars . . . everything that science could ferret out was marked on that map. The known Universe.

'That's what I want,' he breathed. 'Guardian of the Universe!' It was the only position that could sate his burning inner ambitions.

'Surely Trantis will be first, after the Daleks?' Karlton said, softly.

Chen spun around. 'Trantis?' he mocked. 'Trantis? They don't like him.'

'Agreed. But his *is* the largest galaxy.'

Chen dismissed the thought with a wave of the hand. 'He is already demanding too much say in what goes on,' he explained, oblivious to the fact that such were his own demands. 'They want him out of the way. And I have a plan which may help them to achieve their goal. Then it will be I, Mavic Chen, who will be next in line!'

'And I,' Karlton reminded him, 'will be there behind you.'

'Of course,' Chen agreed.

'Of course.' Karlton knew that he would be behind Chen only as long as Chen didn't feel threatened by the presence of another. It would be up to him to assuage Chen's doubts as long as possible.

Chen abruptly came back to the present. 'Is your special force dealing with Vyon?'

'Not directly. I thought it would be wiser to use some of the ordinary security men.'

'Very good,' Chen approved with a smile, taking his seat again. 'You're learning. Who's in command?'

'Kingdom.'

Chen's eyes lit up in appreciation. 'Kingdom! Splendid! A thoroughly reliable agent with an impressive record.'

Karlton smiled. 'And a tendency to shoot first. I thought you'd approve.'

'I do. I would like a private word with Kingdom, please.'

'I thought you might.' Karlton bent forward and triggered the intercom. 'Have agent Kingdom report to Mavic Chen's office immediately.'

Chen stared off at the door, across the luxurious room. The carpet was rich and thick, the paintings on the walls were originals from a dozen worlds. The sculptures were all his own choices from the museums of Earth. Being Guardian of the Solar System had a few good aspects to it. 'I have one or two special instructions for dealing with Bret Vyon,' he mused.

'Is that any better?' Steven asked, finishing winding on the bandage he had found in one of the cupboards.

Bret winced, and tried to stand again. 'It helps. But it still hurts like crazy,' he admitted. His trouser leg was torn open, and the bandage was already slightly bloodstained from the gash on his leg.

The Doctor stopped his pacing back and forth for a moment. 'It's your own wretched fault, young man,' he snapped, most unsympathetically. 'If you had landed that ship in a workmanlike fashion, then you wouldn't be suffering.'

'I did my best, Doctor,' Bret snarled back, stung by the unfair criticism.

'Yes, indeed,' the Doctor retorted. 'Still, I should have known better than to expect a degree of skill from a member of the younger generation. Every one of them fails you when you need them, and then tells you they did their best!'

This was so grossly unfair that Bret's anger drained away. He realized that the Doctor's irritation was merely masking his impatience. 'I got you back to Earth, didn't I?'

'Yes – and almost put us six feet under it!'

Steven gestured around the office that they were waiting in. Bret had directed them here through the security screen about the buildings. 'I still can't see why we're hanging around in here. Can't we just go ahead and inform the Government about the Daleks and have done with it?'

Bret sighed. 'I wish both of you would stop getting at me. Look, if Mavic Chen is in on this with the Daleks, he can hardly be alone. He's also the greatest power in the Solar System. If we're to get help in taking him on, I have to know who will be on our side and who will be on his.'

The Doctor could see the sense in that. 'So, how do you propose to do that?'

Thankful that his companions were listening at last instead of shouting, Bret began to explain. 'This place is an experimental rocket research station. Probing new ways of discovering things. The man in charge here is an old college friend of mind. We've known one another for years. He's a very responsible man in the Government, and he can help us to get our hearing. Daxter is probably the only man who will believe our story.'

The Doctor and Steven had been concentrating on listening to Bret. They were not aware that the door was open until another voice asked: 'What story?'

Chen studied the map on his desk top very carefully. 'The ship came down out here?' he asked.

'That's right,' Karlton explained. 'We've a security team

115

heading out there now. Kingdom can join it when we have the cordon thrown up.'

'Excellent.' The doorway at the end of the room opened, and an agent stepped in. 'Kingdom!' Chen called, warmly. 'Do come in!' He strode around his desk, moving out to meet her.

She walked across the carpet, full of self-confidence. Her eyes flickered around, and Chen knew that she was probably taking in all the details of the room with a glance – truly a born warrior! He examined her carefully. Though he had heard of her, this was the first time he had ever met her. She reminded him of a tightly coiled spring – ready to leap in any direction at an instant's notice.

She was dressed in the inevitable black catsuit that all SSS agents wore, accentuating her perfect figure. She was beautiful, but it was the beauty of ice or steel. Her hair was shoulder-length, and curled inwards. Her face was somewhat elfin. If she smiled, Chen knew she would be considered very desirable. He could not imagine her smiling. Her blue-grey eyes gave back no warmth. She looked every inch the perfect killing machine that her record had informed him she was.

'It's good to see you, Kingdom,' he purred.

There was no flicker of emotion at this. She looked as though meeting the most important man in the Solar System was an everyday event. 'Thank you, sir.'

'I understand that Karlton here has briefed you?'

'Yes, sir.'

'And, naturally, you understand that the capture of these traitors is a matter of the . . . utmost discretion? It would reflect very badly on Special Security if it became known that one of their agents had become a traitor to the human race.'

Kingdom stared steadily at him. 'I understand.'

'In fact,' Chen said, slowly and carefully, 'it would be better for all concerned if the traitors were not to stand trial . . .'

She stared at him again, and supplied what he seemed reluctant to say. 'You don't want them brought in alive.'

116

Chen appreciated this. He chuckled. 'You have a very direct approach to life, Miss Kingdom.'

'And to death,' Karlton added.

She understood these men perfectly. 'You'd prefer the report to state that they were killed attempting to escape.'

'Most succinct and positive,' Chen approved. 'How will you go about locating the traitors?'

'I know where they will be,' Kingdom answered.

Chen was astonished. 'Really?'

'Yes.' For a brief second, some emotion crossed her face, but it was so swift, Chen might have been mistaken to think he saw anything there. She continued: 'I know all about agent Vyon and his background. He will be in the experimental plant.'

Inclining his head, Chen said: 'I see that we were right to entrust you with this mission. There is just one thing more.' He held out his hands, about ten inches apart. 'One of them will be carrying a small device about so long. It is a machine containing Taranium. It is essential that this is recovered intact and returned directly to me. You understand?'

She asked no questions. 'Of course. All precautions for its safety will be taken. Now, with your permission?'

Chen waved his hand magnanimously. 'By all means. I look forward to seeing you again shortly – with the Taranium core and the report of a few – ah – unfortunate deaths.'

Kingdom spun on her heels and marched out of the door. As it slid closed behind her, Chen lowered himself into his seat. He looked appreciatively at Karlton. 'An excellent choice. She is a very direct young woman. It seems a pity that she cannot join our special group.'

Karlton's expression showed an interest in Kingdom that was not strictly business. 'No chance of that?'

'No,' Chen said, reluctantly. He had never felt the attraction of women himself. They wanted a share of power, and Mavic Chen had no intention of sharing anything with anyone. 'The Daleks insist that only fifty humans will be allowed to survive. She'll just have to perish with the rest. Pity, though.'

'Shall I contact the Daleks and inform them of progress?'

'No,' Chen smiled. 'Let's give it another hour. It will be so much better to report in when Vyon is dead and we have the core in our hands.'

Daxter had been introduced to the Doctor and Steven, and listened quietly to their entire story without comment. He was in his early fifties, and obviously a man accustomed to power and authority. He had made a few notes on his pocket computer as the Doctor and Bret had told their story, but refrained from interrupting at any point. When they stopped talking, he looked at them all, thoughtfully. 'I find it hard to believe that Mavic Chen is a traitor.'

'It's true,' Bret insisted. 'He's made some sort of deal with the Daleks. The Doctor saw him talking with them.'

'Is this true?' Daxter asked.

'Quite true,' the Doctor informed him. 'It seems that the Daleks aim to destroy or capture the whole of the Solar System. They have some kind of a weapon that they call the Time Destructor, and Mavic Chen supplied the final part for the machine.'

Daxter shook his head. 'I still can't believe it,' he exclaimed. 'Mavic Chen a traitor!'

'Well, you'd better start believing it,' Steven snapped. 'A very brave girl sacrificed her life while we were bringing this information to Earth. Nothing can make up for her death, but I'd like to think it wasn't entirely wasted!' He shot a filthy look at Bret.

'Quite, quite,' the Doctor said, covering this emotional outburst.

'But why?' Daxter asked. 'Why should Mavic Chen be co-operating with the Daleks?'

'Because he's hungry for power!' the Doctor snapped. 'He's the supreme force in the Solar System, but this is not enough for the man. He wants Universal power.'

'We're going to have to move quickly on this, Daxter,' Bret urged his friend.

'Yes, of course!' Daxter snapped out of his lethargy. 'It will be a vast operation. We'll have to start assembling a fleet to attack Kembel. It's going to take some planning. And we have to get Chen impeached . . .'

This was the stage where the Doctor took his farewells. He knew that he and Steven were now no longer essential to the safety of the Solar System. Humans had many faults, but once they were convinced of the need for action, they could be most forceful. It was time for him to leave. 'Whatever your plans,' he interrupted, 'it is essential that Steven and I return to Kembel. I must recover something of unique value.'

For a moment, there was an expression of horror on Daxter's face. 'You didn't leave the Taranium there?'

'Of course not,' the Doctor snorted. 'But I did leave a piece of very valuable personal property there. We must recover it.'

Relieved, Daxter nodded. 'Of course. We'll see what can be done.'

The Doctor moved carefully away from Daxter, edging closer to Bret. Then he called: 'Steven! Restrain him!'

Steven didn't understand, but he did as the Doctor commanded, and grabbed hold of Daxter. Daxter looked wildly around. 'What are you doing?'

'Yes,' Bret said, coldly. 'What are you doing, Doctor? What kind of a fool game are you playing?'

'Ask Mr Daxter what kind of a fool game *he's* playing.'

'Me?' Daxter spluttered.

'Yes, you,' the Doctor mocked. 'Just what is Mavic Chen paying you for this piece of treachery?'

Puzzled, Bret said: 'He's no traitor. I've known him all my life.'

'It's a stupid assumption,' the Doctor replied, 'that long acquaintance is a guarantee of honesty.'

'But . . . but I'm no traitor,' Daxter said. 'You know that Bret. I'm not a traitor.'

'Oh, you're not, indeed?' The Doctor stuck a finger into Daxter's face. 'Then tell me this: how did you know that the core to the Time Destructor was made of Taranium, eh?'

119

All the colour drained from Daxter's face. He saw the accusing finger, and then Bret's face turned quite cold.

'Yes,' he asked, thinking back. 'How did you know?'

'One of you mentioned it,' Daxter said, wildly. 'While you were telling the story.'

'No,' the Doctor answered. 'None of us did. We didn't mention the core at all, in fact. *You* did.'

Daxter realized that he had been discovered, and that there was no use continuing to play the innocent any longer. He lashed backwards with his foot, hitting Steven hard on the shin. As Steven yelled, Daxter twisted free and ran for the door.

He never made it. Bret had drawn his pistol and fired before Daxter had gone six feet. A brief glow illuminated the man, and he collapsed, dead, to the carpet.

Angrily, the Doctor whirled around. 'How many times do I have to tell you about taking lives?' he exclaimed. 'There were other ways of dealing with him.'

Bret reholstered his gun. 'He deserved worse.'

'Quite so,' the Doctor agreed. 'But now we shall never know whom we can trust!'

The conference room on Kembel had a very tense atmosphere. Though no official meeting had been called, most of the delegates had got into the habit of spending their time there. Trantis, above all, would stand and stare greedily at the map of the Solar System for long periods.

The Black Dalek noted this carefully. Humanoids were so predictable, so hungry for power. Yet they used it for so foolish an end! Power for the Daleks was simply a means to an end – the total subjugation of the Universe to the Dalek will. Their allies at this conference were purely temporary, however deluded the delegates might be on their importance. The only way to subjugate the Universe to the Dalek will was to ensure that the Daleks were the only species left alive in it . . .

The door to the control room hissed open, and a Dalek moved to join the Black Dalek. 'A report from Earth,' it stated. 'Mavic Chen has almost recaptured the Taranium core, and will return here with it in two days.'

'Have the ones who stole it been exterminated?'

'The report did not say.' The Dalek's eye-stick swivelled to take in Trantis. 'But it is believed they were working under the leadership of Trantis.'

'What?' Trantis spun around, his face dark with anger. 'That is not true! It is a lie concocted by Mavic Chen. He is jealous of my power in the outer galaxies!'

That was only too plausible to the Black Dalek. On the other hand, truth was whatever was useful in a given situation – and Trantis was becoming a problem with his continual demands and posturing. Mavic Chen's accusation could be 'proven' if it became necessary to destroy Trantis . . . as Mavic Chen well knew. Chen was proving to be a dangerously intelligent ally. 'We shall see,' the Black Dalek finally stated. 'Has the report been confirmed?'

'No,' the messenger answered. 'It was a suspicion only.'

'It's Mavic Chen!' Trantis insisted. 'He's trying to undermine the galactic council with his accusations!'

'When Mavic Chen returns, we shall discover the truth.' The Black Dalek was totally impassive, as ever. 'Then those who stole the Taranium core will have been identified and exterminated.'

'Now what are we going to do?' Steven asked.

'I don't know,' the Doctor said, thinking furiously. 'But I do think we'd be well advised to get away from here.' He gestured to the body on the floor. 'It's quite likely that Daxter here will be missed very shortly.'

'Good idea,' Bret approved. He levered himself to his feet, and stood, a little uncertainly, on his injured leg.

Steven looked concerned. 'Are you going to be able to walk with that leg of yours?'

'I'll manage,' the agent answered. 'We can get out through the experimental sector. It's usually pretty quiet there, and there are groundcars parked outside. I can probably override one of their computers. It'll speed up our escape.'

'Right,' Steven agreed. 'Let's go.' He walked over to the door, and hit the control to open it. The door hissed aside.

'Hello, Bret.' Kingdom stood in the doorway, her gun at the ready.

After a second of shock, Bret exclaimed: 'Sara!' He gave a sigh of relief, and a slight smile. 'Am I glad to see you. I was beginning to think there was no one I could trust.'

Sara had not returned his smile. On the contrary, her gun never wavered for an instant. Icily, she snapped: 'I don't suppose traitors have a lot of friends.'

Bret couldn't believe what she was saying. He groped for words, but none came. The one person he had been certain would help!

She held out her hand. 'The Taranium,' she said, softly. 'Give it to me.'

A sick feeling overwelmed Bret, and he sagged visibly. 'You, too?' he asked, dully. 'You, too?'

Impatiently, Sara moved forward, aiming to search Bret for the core – not realizing that the Doctor had it. As she moved, Steven grabbed his chance. He jumped at her, and smashed aside her arm before she could retrain the gun on him. Then he threw her as hard as he could across the room.

'Come on,' he yelled. 'Run for it!'

The Doctor needed no further urging. Together, the two of them dashed into the corridor and away. Bret, hampered by his injured leg, was a little slower. In the doorway, he paused, looking back at Sara, still finding the fact that she was also one of the traitors hard to accept.

Sara had been slightly dazed by the force of the blow, but she shook her head, and staggered back to her feet. What a stupid move! She had been so intent on Bret that she had neglected to watch the other two men carefully enough! She dived for her pistol, and then dashed to the door. Bret was still in sight, limping down the corridor. She brought up her gun and aimed it.

'Stay where you are!' she called, fighting to keep her voice level. She knew what her orders were, but it was simpler to think about killing Bret than actually to do it.

Her finger tightened on the trigger, and Bret refused to stop.

She fired, closing her eyes at the last second. She heard the thud of Bret's body hitting the floor, and then she opened her eyes and looked. He was down, but not quite dead. Sara hurried over to him, and turned him gently on his back.

His eyes were open, and filled with pain. It was more than physical pain – though that must have been extreme, and it was astonishing that he was still clinging to life. 'How?' he whispered. 'How could . . . Mavic Chen . . . have bought you? How?' His will could not hold his wrecked body together any longer. With a sigh, he died.

Sara laid him gently to the floor, fighting back the emotion that threatened to wash over her. She also held back from thinking about Bret's last words. There were still two intruders to kill.

Steven and the Doctor dashed past a sign that warned special passes were needed to enter the next area. The last thing on their minds at the moment was approval for their various trespasses. They ran through the only door opening from the corridor.

They were in a perfectly blank room. Its white walls were devoid of features, and there was no other way out. The only thing in the room besides themselves was a strange-looking machine about the size of a man, and vaguely pyramid-shaped.

'No time to retrace out steps,' the Doctor gasped. All this exercise was quite fatiguing. At his age, he shouldn't be expected to run all the time. 'Let's hope that woman thinks we've gone elsewhere.'

Steven closed the door. 'Did you see anything of Bret?' he asked, softly. The Doctor shook his head. Steven was worried, but there was no way of checking on their friend without the risk of running into that other agent. 'Well,' Steven whispered finally, 'what do we do now?'

From the expression on the Doctor's face, the same question was going through his mind also. There was no need for him to answer, because at that moment the door opened.

Sara stood in the doorway, gun in hand. The two men stared at her in amazement. What idiots! Did they think they could escape her heat sensors by running? She brought her weapon to cover them both. 'You are trying to escape,' she said, flatly. 'That means I shall have to kill you.'

12

Counter-plot

In another room of the experimental complex, Froyn and Rhymnal eagerly exchanged delighted smiles. Both men had been working for several years on a particularly tricky and delicate experimental procedure – which was finally about to be tested for the first time. Both men hovered around a central panel in a room lined with computers. Even with the sophisticated machines of the year AD 4000, the amount of calculating needed to get this experiment perfect was staggering. Vast rows of humming computers worked through the figures, projections, energy requirements and safety margins. The expenditure of energy alone in this experiment was horrendously high – Froyn had often quipped that he was glad it wouldn't be on his personal debit. Only the Government of the Solar System could ever have afforded even to think about trying this experiment.

Rhymnal checked the final couplings, and smiled. 'Power flow is at maximum,' he reported for posterity. Naturally, they were recording the whole experiment. Everything was looking good.

'All instrumentation is green,' Froyn added. 'Starting transmitter.' He hit the controls for this, and then nodded. 'Transmitter functioning perfectly.'

Powering up another panel, Rhymnal said: 'Disseminators active. Cellular charge projecting is holding steady.'

Taking a deep breath, Froyn sat at the final control panel. It was all looking excellent. 'Countdown commencing. Ten, nine . . .'

In their featureless room, the Doctor and Steven were completely at the mercy of Sara Kingdom. 'Right,' she said, 'I'll give you five seconds to hand over the Taranium.'

Neither of the men moved, and Sara took a step forward. At that second, the pyramid-shaped machine in the centre of the room sprang to life. Though they could not know it, the three of them were watching the transmitter powering up. They were actually standing in the room where Froyn and Rhymnal's experiment was to be conducted. In some bewilderment, Sara glanced nervously around. The featureless walls suddenly began to pulse with an inner fire.

Sara spun around, but the door through which she had entered was locked. The roof now began to pulse with the mysterious light, and then everything suddenly went white. She felt as though every fibre of her body was being stretched, strained and snapped. Awash with pain, her consciousness evaporated.

'High negative absorption,' Froyn reported, as the power discharge sent through the experimental chamber began to fall. 'Power down now.'

Rhymnal was having a difficult time keeping a smile from his face. Scientific detachment! he reminded himself. 'Projection wave is in synchronization with target figures.' He could barely keep the excitement out of his voice. 'All instruments show perfect dissemination.'

Nodding, Froyn shunted in the electronic brains. 'All controls now on to computer monitoring.' He sat back, and let out a whoop of sheer joy.

Rhymnal's face cracked from side to side in a huge smile. 'Perfect,' he crowed. 'Absolutely perfect!'

'Like a dream,' Froyn agreed. He switched on a monitor, which showed the room in which Sara had confronted the Doctor and Steven. It was perfectly empty now. The walls and roof had returned to their normal white state. The transmitter had also vanished.

The two men had very little to do for this stage of the experiment, but neither of them could simply sit still and wait. They occupied themselves taking totally unnecessary readings that showed the energy beam was functioning exactly in accordance with their computer projections. As they worked, the door opened.

Annoyed at the interruption, Froyn glanced up. 'Who the devil are you, and who let you in here?' he demanded.

The man was dressed in black, and carried a gun in his hand. He was dark, tall and muscular, but his face looked distinctly worried. He flashed a computer ID card at them. 'Borkar,' he snapped. 'SSS.' He gestured back over his shoulder. 'That room down the corridor there – what's going on? I can't get into it.'

'You're not supposed to get into it,' Rhymnal replied, angrily. 'That's why there are all those "Keep out" notices plastered all over the walls. Now, kindly go away and leave us alone. We're in the middle of a very sensitive experiment – which has already been cleared by security.'

'I don't much care what you're in the middle of,' Borkar said, coldly. 'This is a security matter now.'

Rhymnal sighed in exasperation. Just like the security people to start getting fussy right in the middle of the crucial phase of their operations! They'd probably neglected to fill out some obscure form in triplicate a month ago, and the loss had just been noted. Typical. 'Look, what's this got to do with the cellular projector?'

'Your what? I don't care about projectors – I want to know about that room. One of our agents went into it, chasing a couple of suspects.'

'What?' Both Froyn and Rhymnal suddenly looked horrified, the blood draining from their faces.

'I'm her back-up,' Borkar explained. 'When I tried to open the door, it was shut fast. Then there was some kind of a power surge. I followed the passage down to here.'

The two scientists exchanged very worried looks. Rhymnal finally asked: 'You say that there were people inside the projector?'

'Projector?' Borkar still had no idea what they were talking about. 'There are three people inside that room, and the door is locked. Two of them are very dangerous criminals. Now, throw your switches or whatever you do and unseal those doors so that I can get inside and help my leader.'

Rhymnal shook his head, slowly, still trying to comprehend the magnitude of this disaster. 'It wouldn't do any good, I'm afraid. The projector has already been activated.'

'What the devil are you talking about?' Borkar yelled.

Froyn answered him, softly. 'What we mean is that anyone who was inside that room is no longer in there. It's a cellular projector, and everything that was inside that room is being transmitted through space.'

Helpfully, Rhymnal aded: 'They're part of a wave-front of energy that is travelling through our Galaxy at many times the speed of light. They're billions of miles from here now – if they are still alive.'

The delays were becoming quite irritating now. The Black Dalek spun to face the communications technician again. 'Is there any further report from Mavic Chen?'

'No.' The technician examined its panel. 'There has been none now for over two hours.'

Trantis felt elated by this news. 'Perhaps,' he suggested, carefully, 'Mavic Chen erred when he told you that he could recover the Taranium core – as he erred when he suggested that my people were behind the theft?'

The Black Dalek had no time for the petty feuds of these foolish humanoids. 'Mavic Chen will recover the core,' it stated firmly. 'Failure to do so will lead to his immediate extermination.'

'That could be a trifle difficult,' Trantis pointed out. 'After all, the Guardian of the Solar System is on Earth now – and out of reach of your weapons.'

The eye-stick spun to focus on him. 'Nowhere is out of reach of the Daleks,' the Black Dalek grated, ominously. 'We repay failure with death. Do not forget that. Ever.'

Trantis huddled deeper into the shadows, knowing that he had been given his own warning – and that there would be no more.

The laboratory was becoming quite crowded by now. Borkar had made a short report over his communicator to his superiors. Karlton and Mavic Chen had arrived as swiftly as they could, to the disgust of Froyn and Rhymnal. The two men simply wanted to continue with their readings. Three people in that room had added mass they hadn't taken into account when they had powered up the transfer beam. Who knew what it might have done to their experiment?

Mavic Chen's view of the situation was far different. He eyed agent Borkar in barely contained fury. 'I understand that you let the traitors escape!' he accused.

'Well, not exactly,' Borkar said, carefully. Answering in person for failure to the Guardian was not a way calculated to get an agent promotion. 'You see . . .'

Cutting him off, Chen demanded: 'Do you have them or not?'

'No, sir.'

Chen looked at him angrily, then bit back his wrath. 'Very well. Give me your report.'

Smartly, Borkar did so. 'Sir, I was back-up to agent Kingdom. She killed the traitor Vyon, then pursued the two remaining suspects into what we both believed was a normal room. When I attempted to follow to assist her, the door was locked.' He gestured at the two scientists, who were struggling to get around the other men in the room to take their readings. 'These men can best explain what happened next, sir.'

Chen rounded on Froyn and Rhymnal; Borkar was glad to be out of the heat for the moment. 'Well?'

'It's an experimental space travel system,' Froyn explained, glad to have got the ear of the Guardian of the Solar System. 'As you know, we've been using T-mat beams for centuries to travel through the Solar System, but longer distances have eluded us. Our system should break the distance barriers.'

'I don't want a lecture,' Chen said impatiently. 'I just want to know where the three people are now.'

'Well,' Rhymnal offered, 'if they survived the cellular structural change, then they should be approaching the pre-set destination.'

You couldn't get a straight answer from a scientist. Chen raised an eyebrow and prompted: 'And that is?'

'The planet Mira.'

That was all Chen needed – some obscure planet half a Galaxy away! He slammed his fist into his palm in annoyance. There had to be some way out of this – there had to be! He turned back to the two scientists. 'And what are the chances that they are still alive?'

Froyn glanced at his companion, who nodded encouragingly. 'Well, according to our instruments, everything functioned perfectly, despite the excess mass that we had not calculated on.' He dried up under Chen's withering glare, then added, quickly: 'I think it's safe to say that they're alive.'

Thank you,' Chen said, with heavy sarcasm. 'Please leave us for a moment.' The two scientists shrugged, picked up their notes and wandered out into the corridor to confer on how this would affect their experiments, and the results. Chen stared pointedly at Borkar. 'You too.'

When he was finally alone with Karlton, Chen whirled around to face his assistant. 'Mira is not far from Kembel, is it?'

Karlton shrugged. 'It's nearer than Earth is.'

Chen nodded, a plan having already formed in his Machiavellian mind. 'We'll have to call the Daleks and tell them about this. Tell the Daleks that you tricked the fugitives into the cellular transporter deliberately.'

Karlton stared at him. 'You think they'll believe it?'

'Of course they will believe it! They imagine that no one would ever dare to lie to them deliberately. Make them believe that we planned it so that they could personally recover the core faster this way around. It will suit their plans, and they will naturally believe it.'

Karlton nodded, thoughtfully. 'Anything else?'

'Yes. Have a ship made ready for me.' Chen looked pained for a moment. 'I do wish that idiot Vyon hadn't wrecked my *Spar* . . . Ah well, you can't conquer a Universe without a few losses.'

'Where will you be going?'

'Back to Kembel. It might be better if I were on hand when the Daleks recover the Taranium core.'

That made sense to Karlton. 'I'll invent a cover story to explain your absence,' he said. 'When will you return to Earth?'

'I shan't,' Chen replied. 'It's too close to the limit now. I shall stay on Kembel until the Daleks begin their master-plan. You and the others will be able to join me there in about three weeks.'

Thinking about his plans always pleased Mavic Chen. The Daleks thought that they were using him, but they didn't dream of how grandly Chen had planned! With the Dalek taskforce heading towards Earth in three weeks, Kembel would be left vulnerable to a small strike fleet . . . 'The day of Armageddon is drawing close,' Chen breathed, savouring his plans. 'The whole history of mankind will be snuffed out like a candle in the wind. When I return to the Earth it will be with a power that no human has ever known! Power absolute!' The inner light of madness was burning strongly now, and Karlton knew better than to interrupt. 'Then Earth will rise again, but without the shackles of infantile philosophies like democracy and equal-ity! It will be a new and virgin land that can be shaped . . . moulded . . . fashioned into the image that *I* design. *I* will be its life-blood – *I* its creator – *I* its very god!'

Abruptly, Chen seemed to realize where he was, and he slowly calmed down, his vision burning dimmer. After a moment, he turned to his assistant. 'You are a fortunate man, Karlton,' he observed in quieter tones. 'You will have a high place in this destiny.'

'The highest,' Karlton agreed, obsequiously. 'Next to you.'

'Yes,' Chen said, thoughtfully. Was this fool getting ideas above his station? Could Chen continue to trust him for much longer? 'But now there is much to be done. Contact the Daleks and tell them that the fugitives are ready for them on Mira . . .'

* * *

131

Tendrils of mist curled through the lianas that festooned the huge trees. Low-lying, stagnant pools were interspersed by the trees, whose thick, woody roots protruded from the stinking ground. Ferns and feather-like plants grew in uneven clumps. Insect-like creatures buzzed and zipped through the heavy, oppressive air. Dank smells came and went, carried by what little breezes there were.

It was hot and oppressive. It was smelly and unpleasant. It was the surface of the planet Mira.

The everglade-like trees shadowed out much of the sun, so it was difficult to see too far. Dead plants, falling into the waters, rotted where they lay. Occasionally, bubbles of marsh gas broke the surface, hardly improving the quality of the air.

Close by one such unhealthy pool lay the Doctor. He was on a small hill rising from the waters, and close behind him was a small cave, worn from the rocks by the water action of the swamps over the centuries. Around the Doctor's unconscious form were scattered various straggly bushes, overlaid by hairy creepers, and overshadowed by the huge trees.

One of the creepers swung aside, and the leaves of the bush rustled. Had there been a wind, this would not have been remarkable. Since the air was still, though, there was no apparent explanation for the movements. Then the branches of the bush moved, and there was an audible crack as dead material snapped under the weight of something.

Apart from the Doctor, though, the clearing was quite empty.

The ground by the Doctor was wet and muddy. Had the old man been awake, he would have viewed with considerable interest – and probably a little trepidation – the footprints that formed in the mud. There was nothing apparently there to cause them. They were the markings of large, bird-like claws.

Laboured breathing was coming from a spot about seven feet from the ground. It sounded as if a heavy creature was breathing through some form of membrane, and having a

132

good deal of difficulty managing it. This noise moved closer to the Doctor as the invisible being producing it bent to examine this intruder.

'Ugly,' a voice whispered. The creature reached out and lifted one of the Doctor's arms, then let it fall. Invisible fingers traced the form of the Doctor's face. Invisible organs of sight surveyed what they could see. The creature – a Visian – didn't care for the alien intruder. There was little enough food to be found in this swamp as it was, and fierce competition for what was there with all native life-forms. The last thing the Visians wanted was a new species moving in to take some of that precious food.

Then again, maybe this new creature was edible?

The Visian paused to study the Doctor again, and to pinch at the flesh. Thin, very thin. Not good feasting here.

The Doctor groaned. The invisible creature jumped back, splashing in a puddle as it did so. The Doctor began to stir, finally waking. Deciding that discretion was perhaps the most admirable virtue, the Visian beat a hasty retreat to the safety of the bushes. There it lurked, watching unseen as the Doctor groaned again and finally managed to lever himself into a sitting position.

His head was aching slightly, and a dreadful smell assaulted his nostrils, acting like smelling salts. Shaking his head to clear away the vestiges of unconsciousness, the Doctor wearily clambered to his feet. Not for the first time, he wished he still had one of his walking sticks from the TARDIS with him. This ground looked quite treacherous indeed.

There was no sign of his companions, nor of the room in which they had been standing. 'Not the Earth,' the Doctor muttered, looking about. 'Even that planet doesn't smell this foul.' He batted at the air in front of his face, making no discernible difference to the stench. Giving up, he called: 'Steven! Steven!'

There was no reply. Shrugging to himself, the Doctor chose a direction at random to start searching for his young friend. He had taken only a step when he spotted the footprints left by the visitor hiding in the bushes. He went down on to one knee, investigating the print with great care. It was already starting to fill with water, but it told him a few things. 'Tall,' he deduced. 'About seven feet, I should say. Heavy, too, and bipedal. Good length of stride. Quite formidable, I imagine. And *fresh*,' he added, seeing the rate at which water was seeping into his own footprints. The creature that had made these prints couldn't have gone far. The Doctor examined the landscape carefully, but saw nothing, even though the Visian was hunched less than twelve feet away from him.

The Doctor set off into the bushes, beginning a slow sweep of the area. After a moment, the Visian stood up. It followed, quietly and invisibly, after the Doctor. Footprints appeared as it walked, and the bushes moved when it pushed them aside. Otherwise, there was nothing to show its passage.

It took about five minutes for the Doctor to find Steven. The young man was lying on the grass, looking almost peaceful. Shaking his head, the Doctor hurried over. 'Steven!' he called urgently into his companion's ear. 'Steven!' He helped the young pilot to sit up and, eventually, Steven began to come round.

'What happened?' he asked, rubbing the back of his head, which pained him. He took in the surroundings, and then the Doctor. 'She . . . she was going to shoot . . . to shoot . . . what happened?'

'I'm not entirely sure,' the Doctor confessed. 'If she *did* shoot, though, I don't think we've come to Katarina's Place of Perfection, judging by the surroundings and the smell.'

'Phew,' Steven agreed. 'It's like a hothouse in here. Where are we?'

'I really don't have the faintest idea,' the Doctor replied cheerfully. 'One minute we were in a room on the Earth, and the next – here.' He waved an arm about.

Steven was trying to get his thoughts together. 'I seem to remember falling,' he said, slowly. 'As if I were falling a long distance. It's vague, though. Maybe it was just a dream.'

The Doctor patted his arm. 'I seem to have experienced

something of the same dream, then. However, *how* we got here isn't all that important. What we do need to know is *where* we are. Do you recall that machine that stood in the centre of the room with us? I suspect that it was some form of transmitter, and that it will be with us here somewhere. We can be certain that however we were projected to this place, they will know about it on the Earth. That means that Mavic Chen will know – and so will the Daleks!'

Their thoughts were cut off by the sound of a woman's scream.

13

Allies

'Come on!' Steven yelled, and started off through the bushes in the direction of the scream. It had been filled with terror, then abruptly cut off. The Doctor did his best in the enervating atmosphere to keep up with the far younger man. Neither of them cared too much about the obvious conclusion that it had to have been the woman who had tried to kill them who was in trouble.

They broke into a small clearing, and stopped in astonishment.

Sara Kingdom was being held, a kicking struggling captive – but there was *nothing* there. Her feet were several inches off the ground, and her mouth contorted, as though something was pressed upon it. Her arms were shaking, struggling with something. It would have looked almost comical, had it not been deadly serious.

The two Visians that had grabbed Sara were attempting to drag her back to their main encampment a couple of miles through the swamps. Suddenly, they saw two more of the same ugly creatures appear, and the odds no longer seemed so fine. They could not be seen directly, but these new arrivals would be able to guess where they were from where Sara was being restrained. With one accord, the Visians dropped Sara and fled into the bushes.

Sara hit the ground with a squelch. Two arms caught at her, and she started to struggle again. Then she realized that she could see these arms, and that they were attached to a handsome-looking man who was trying to help her regain her feet. Gratefully, she accepted the help, and stood there, shuddering.

'It was horrible,' she gasped. 'I couldn't see anything,

but I was enveloped . . . It touched me, and . . .' Her body shook, and Steven held on to her, comforting her. It wasn't a hardship for him, considering how pretty she was. She didn't seem to recognize him at all.

The Doctor moved over and examined her with a twinkle in his eye. 'This is an interesting change in our situation, eh, young woman?' He peered down his nose into her puzzled face. 'It seems like it was only minutes ago that you were trying to gun us down in cold blood.'

The shock finally left Sara, and she understood in sudden fury who these two strangers were. Angrily, she tore herself from Steven's arms, and her hand went automatically to her holster. 'The traitors!' she exclaimed. Her gun was gone, and nowhere to be seen.

Taking no apparent notice of her hostile actions, the Doctor continued as cheerfully as before. 'Well, of course you needn't hang about with such terrible specimens as us.' He waved his hand at the bushes. 'You could always run along into the jungle, if you like,' he added, helpfully. 'I'm sure we won't stop you. I should think you may get an – ah – enthusiastic welcome out there.'

Sara took one look at the bushes, and shuddered again. Those cold, clammy claws that had grabbed at her before were out there, unseen, and waiting. She took a nervous step back towards the two men, then stopped, caught in indecision.

'Whatever you may think of us,' Steven said, 'I think we're a better alternative than what is waiting out there.'

'Shall we join forces?' the Doctor suggested. 'A truce to get us away from this place?'

Sara considered the matter as rationally as she could. She knew that her fear of the invisible creatures was unbalancing her slightly, but she simply couldn't face them alone again. Besides, if she stayed with these two characters, she'd be able to keep track of them for when the upper hand passed back to her – as it inevitably would. 'All right,' she agreed. 'But it doesn't change anything. My orders are to kill you, and I aim to carry out your execution once we're away from here.'

Steven snorted. 'Well, I hope you've no objection if we try to avoid being killed.'

'You won't think it's so funny once we're out of here,' Sara warned him.

The Doctor smiled, cheerfully. 'Now, let's not get off to a bad start for this alliance by squabbling, shall we? I think we'd first best get to firmer ground. There was a cave back over that way that should make a passable camp. Come along, come along.' Leading the way with confidence, he started out, reversing his path. Steven and Sara, eyeing one another warily, followed behind him.

After a moment, the first Visian turned to its companion. 'Summon more of the People,' he breathed. 'These strange invaders cannot be tolerated. They must be destroyed, so that no more follow. There is not room here for our People and these ugly intruders.'

There was a rustling of the bushes as the first Visian's companion sped away, back to their camp. Satisfied, the remaining creature started to follow the strange intruders.

The Dalek control room on Kembel was once again operating at maximum efficiency. The various Dalek technicians assembled about the machines were working diligently as the Black Dalek entered. It glided to the supervisor and demanded: 'Report!'

The supervisor spun its head section about, as its arm continued to operate the computer controls. 'The pursuit ship is now approaching the planet Mira.'

'You will order the patrol to take the captives alive.'

'I obey.'

'It is vital that the core of the Time Destructor is recovered,' the Black Dalek stated.

'It is possible that the fugitives know of its value to us,' the supervisor replied. 'They may attempt to conceal the core, or bargain for its return.'

This possibility had occurred to the Black Dalek. 'If necessary, we shall agree to the demands of the fugitives. We must recover the core.'

'And then?'

'Bargains with lesser life-forms are not important. The fugitives will then be exterminated.' The Black Dalek spun about and returned to the conference room, where their alien allies were waiting for news.

The monitor Dalek moved to join its supervisor. 'I have contacted the pursuit craft,' it reported. 'They have landed on the planet Mira.'

'Have they located the fugitives?'

'Their perceptors register strong readings at a range of five units.'

'Maintain contact,' the supervisor commanded. 'When they report the capture of the fugitives, inform the Supreme Dalek immediately.'

'I obey.'

On Mira, a patrol of Daleks had set out from their craft, working their way through the narrow pathways of the planet's uneven surface. It was difficult going, owing to the marshy nature of the ground. The Daleks, due to their weight, could move only slowly across large stretches of the virtually nonexistent pathways. Numerous detours round mudholes and large pools of water were necessary.

One of the Daleks was fitted with a perceptor, one of the Daleks' standard tracking devices. It registered movement, and was extremely accurate. Abruptly, the compass-like needle began to register. 'Perceptor recording movement at very close range,' the Dalek reported.

The patrol leader began to scan the area. Its head-section traversed 360 degrees without detecting anything. Switching to infra-red, it tried again, without success. 'No visual contact.'

The perceptor stubbornly insisted that there was a large degree of movement. 'Perceptor registers approaching life-forms,' the tracker insisted. The leader scanned again, still with nothing to show for its efforts. 'Perceptor registers movement in immediate vicinity.'

There was the faintest hint of a bush moving. The patrol leader spun about and fired. The bush and its environs were bathed in lethal radiation. From the air, a hideous shriek registered as the death-cry of something. The patrol leader moved forward to investigate, as it could still see nothing.

It ran directly into that nothing. Puzzled, the Dalek extended its arm. Despite the fact that it could detect nothing visually, something was sprawled across the ground just in front of it. The Dalek ran its visual equipment across its entire spectrum of operations without being able to make anything out. Finally, it turned back to the waiting patrol.

'These creatures are invisible,' it stated. 'Keep constant checks on the perceptor. Open fire when it registers contact. We will proceed.'

Having set up their temporary camp in the small cave, the Doctor kept watch while Steven attempted to set Sara straight about what was really happening. Reluctantly, Sara had forced herself to listen, almost convinced that the story was a tissue of lies. Almost, but not quite. The terrible betrayed expression of Bret as he had died kept coming back to mind.

'I swear, everything I've told you is the truth,' Steven finished, wondering how much had got through to this cold-hearted creature. 'Mavic Chen is the traitor, not us.'

Sara shrugged. 'It's rather hard to accept. Mavic Chen is the most trusted man in the Solar System – and who would take the word of a couple of space travellers over his? I'd need proof of what you say to be convinced of this wild accusation.' She thought for a moment. 'This Taranium core – you still have it?'

'Yes,' said the Doctor. He removed it from his pocket, and showed it to her. The small, glowing device seemed so innocent – and yet how many people had already died to keep it from the Daleks?

'Anyway, it's not important any longer,' Steven said. 'It doesn't matter whether you believe us or not. Bret is on the Earth, and he'll tell the story to the right person.' He didn't see the expression on Sara's face. 'I shouldn't be surprised if he's got a fleet together to blast Kembel right out of the sky.'

'That's not very likely,' Sara said, softly.

'Then you don't know Bret Vyon,' Steven smiled. 'He's pretty efficient and convincing once he gets started. He won't take no for an answer.'

Before Steven could elaborate on Bret's virtues, Sara cut him short. 'Bret won't tell anything to anyone,' she said, flatly. 'He's dead.' Seeing Steven's stunned expression, she added: 'I killed him.'

Even the Doctor had not been prepared for this news. He and Steven looked at one another so despairingly that Sara discovered that she believed their wild story utterly. There was no way that they could have faked that look of terrible loss. Then their accusing eyes turned on her, and she knew she'd been a dreadful fool. 'I didn't know!' she yelled at them. 'I was only obeying my orders! *I didn't know!*' She buried her face in her hands, sobbing, trying to escape those burning eyes, but she couldn't. The eyes that accused her the most were her own.

Steven and the Doctor were at a loss for words, and could offer her no comfort. Finally, Steven said, bleakly: 'This changes things, doesn't it?'

'I'm afraid it does,' the Doctor agreed. 'Now we are the only ones left who can warn the Earth.'

'Warn the Earth!' Steven slammed his fist onto the wall of the cave in frustration. 'Tell me how! We don't even know where we are!'

'We don't need to.'

Puzzled, Steven said: 'I don't understand you.'

With a smile, the Doctor held up the core. 'The Daleks can't go through with their plans without this.'

Elatedly, Steven nodded. 'Of course! It'll take them forever to get enough Taranium to build a replacement core.'

The Doctor shook his head. 'No, my boy, you don't understand the Daleks. They won't give up that simply. They'll track us down and come after us. They'd follow us to the ends of space and time if they had to.'

'Then what do we do?'

'Wait,' said the Doctor. 'Wait until they find us. And

then – out-think them. Beat them at their own game. They'll be coming for us, never doubt it. When they do, we must be ready.' He gripped his lapels, and stared off into the jungle below.

Steven knew that the Doctor's optimism masked his worries. 'The odds are poor,' he observed. 'The two of us and her – ' he indicated the still-sobbing Sara ' – against the might of the Daleks and their allies.'

'The odds are great,' the Doctor agreed. 'But, then, so are the stakes – the life of every man, woman and child on Earth.' After a moment's pause, he added, more practically: 'The sun is going down. I suspect that it will get quite cold when night falls. I'll go and look for some wood to start a fire.' He glanced over at Sara. 'In the meantime, do try to comfort her. Crying women make me most uncomfortable.'

As the Doctor disappeared into the trees, Steven walked carefully over to Sara. He put a gentle arm about her. 'Sara,' he began, but she wrenched away from him – this time not loathing him, but herself.

'Let me alone,' she gasped between sobs. 'Please.' Steven could see that she was fighting an inner battle, but knew that she simply had to be wrenched out of it, or she'd be useless to them.

'Look,' he said, awkwardly, 'it wasn't your fault. Like you said, you were just acting on orders. How could you know that Bret wasn't a traitor when your superiors told you he was?'

She looked up, drawn and haggard. 'I killed him,' she said. 'I just obeyed what they told me without question. I should have known Bret better than to believe he was a traitor. I should have asked questions! I should have doubted!'

'Did . . . did you know Bret?'

'Know him?' She looked as though her life were emptied of meaning. 'He was my brother.'

Mavic Chen looked around his office with considerable regret. He had spent years building up this collection of artwork, and all the power and wealth that it represented.

In a short while, the Daleks would annihilate it all. He would miss these paintings, and the statues, but one had to make sacrifices. He looked up as Karlton entered.

'I have a ship ready for you,' the security man reported.

'Good.' Chen stepped to the window, looking over New Washington. The vast metropolis teamed with life – at least, for now. 'I believe that the Daleks must have reached Mira by now.'

'Yes. It looks as though the Daleks accepted my story.'

'And why shouldn't they?' Chen turned his back on the mass of humanity outside. 'I must be there when the Taranium core is brought back to Kembel.'

'If it is,' Karlton cautioned. 'We don't know that it – and the traitors – survived the transportation to Mira.'

Chen waved the possibility away. 'Those scientists may have been narrow-minded, but they were quite certain that their foolish experiment went satisfactorily. Now, wait until you hear from me. Assemble the force in orbit about Venus. We know the date of the Dalek attack on Earth. When this occurs, the Daleks will be too busy to pay heed to your fleet. Whatever happens, we shall outwit the Daleks.'

Karlton nodded. 'We should be able to destroy Kembel at that time with ease. But that will give us mastery of only this Galaxy.'

Chen put an arm about his assistant's shoulder. 'Karlton, you lack vision. Why do you think I want to be on hand when the Daleks recover the core? I shall be on Kembel, with the Time Destructor. While the Daleks are expending their forces on obliterating the Earth, we shall take possession of the Time Destructor, and turn it on them. With the power of the Time Destructor in our hands, we shall be able to conquer more than this Galaxy – we shall become the masters of the entire Universe!'

The Doctor bustled about in the trees, collecting the wood for kindling a fire. He was by no means certain they would need one, but he had been unable to bear that wretched woman's crying any longer. Overt displays of sentimentality always pained him. He rummaged about for sticks that

143

were dry enough to catch alight – no simple task in this damp place.

There was a slight noise in the bushes ahead, and the Doctor carefully continued his work of collecting wood. His eyes, however, never left the bushes. He found a stick that was about four feet long, and fairly hefty. Dropping his pile of kindling, he used the stick to swipe hard at the bush.

He hit nothing but the leaves, which rustled and gave way. There was a sound of laboured breathing to his right, and he spun about, brandishing his stick. There was more of the rasping breathing from the left, and then from all about him. He was being surrounded by these invisible foes. He lashed out with the stick, only to have something unseen grab it and tear it from his hands. Something jumped at him from behind, and he felt long, thin talons clutching for his throat. The weight of the creature dragged the Doctor to the muddy ground.

Groping about, the Doctor's hands closed about a small rock. Wrenching it free of the mud's sticky embrace, he swung the rock backwards. He was rewarded by the sound and feel of it striking something. A reedy cry burst from the air, and the claws were gone. Staggering to his feet, the Doctor was breathing heavily. In this humidity, any exertions were very tiring. He glared about, waiting for any sounds that might betray one of his attackers.

The Visians had paused as the Doctor had fought. They were not brave by nature, preferring to use their invisibility as a cloak to ambush their food. Still, there were enough of them now to give one another courage. 'Kill the intruder,' the first Visian whispered, in its wet, reedy tones. 'Kill it.'

The rest of the group took up this thought, as they edged in closer to the Doctor. He could see nothing, but their thin voices carried very clearly. 'Kill it . . . kill it . . . kill it . . .'

Nervously, the Doctor began backing away. He bumped into something invisible, and then wrenched himself free. 'Steven!' he yelled. 'Steven!' The forms were closing in about him when he saw Steven dashing on to the scene.

Taking in the sight of the Doctor, standing apparently alone, but hearing the voices chanting, Steven realized that the old man was surrounded by the aliens. He looked about, and saw the stick that the Visians had torn from the Doctor's grip. Taking it up, Steven gave an incoherent yell, and dashed forwards, whipping the stick back and forth.

He was happy when the stick connected with one of the creatures. A mournful wail, then Steven rammed the being with his shoulder. He felt the creature go staggering off. Another invisible enemy screamed and collapsed under a heavy blow from the stick. Then Steven was with the Doctor.

'Capital, my boy, capital!' the Doctor approved. 'Now, let's get out of here.'

Together, they moved forwards. Steven kept the stick whirling, but hit nothing. Clearly the aliens had fallen back under the fury of his assault. With one accord, they dashed back towards the cave.

Left alone by Steven, Sara had glanced nervously through the hanging lianas at the trees below. Then, though the air was still, she saw one of the vines move. There was an alien with her in the cave.

She didn't feel as frightened now as when she had woken in the forest earlier, to find herself attacked by things she couldn't see. Her training had been thorough, and she was mentally prepared for an invisible opponent. Besides, she wasn't as weaponless as she appeared, simply because her blaster was gone. She flicked her right wrist, and a thin knife snapped into her grip from its concealed sheath on her forearm.

The floor of the cave, like almost all of the surface of this world, was partly a pool of mud. Sara saw the markings of a clawed foot suddenly appear at one point, and lunged at that spot with her knife. There was a squawk, and the creature back-pedalled furiously. Sara dashed forward after it, and slipped in the mud. She rolled, fast, in case the creature attacked, and then sprang back to her feet.

There was neither sight nor sound of anything with her in the cave. Sara brushed at the mud on her skin, uncomfortably aware of the fact that her clothes were covered in the stuff. At that moment, the Doctor and Steven came staggering up to the cave mouth. Sawing back and forth with her knife to deter the invisible creature from attacking her, Sara retreated to join them.

'Careful,' she warned them. 'There's one of those things in the cave.'

'Great,' Steven said, pessimistically. 'And there're dozens more of them behind us.'

'What we need to know,' the Doctor said, thoughtfully, looking at Sara's dirty costume, 'is the nature of these creatures. If we knew what they looked like, then perhaps we should perceive some weaknesses in them, mmm?'

'But they're invisible,' objected Sara. 'We can't see them.'

'Perhaps not *them*,' the Doctor agreed with a chuckle. 'But we can see other things. A sheet of glass might be almost invisible, but if you painted it, then you could see it without difficulty.'

Sara caught on quickly. With a delighted grin, she pointed to herself. 'Mud!'

'I don't understand,' Steven objected.

The Doctor's patted him on the arm. 'My dear boy, I don't expect you to. We're a splendid team, you and I. I supply the brains and you supply the brawn. Now, listen, you trust me, don't you?'

'Why do I get a bad feeling about this?'

'Of course you do,' the Doctor said, answering his own question. 'Now, I wouldn't ask you to do anything that was dangerous, would I?'

Steven glared at him, but the Doctor smiled, disarmingly. 'It is vital, young man, that we know what these creatures look like.'

'So what do I have to do?' Steven demanded.

Waving his hand airily, the Doctor said: 'It's nothing, nothing at all. Just go into the cave and tackle that creature.'

'What?' Steven exploded.

'Just drag it out here,' the Doctor amplified. 'Sara and I will do the rest.'

146

'But I could get killed!'

'Killed.' The Doctor looked as though the thought had never occurred to him. Then he shook his head firmly. 'No, I don't think so. I'm almost certain that there's no danger of that. Now, go along with you, there's a good fellow.'

Grinning, Sara added: 'We'll be right here.'

'Thanks a lot!'

'Do hurry up,' the Doctor snapped. 'If you dilly-dally much longer, we'll have the rest of them on our necks, too.'

Steven took a deep breath and stepped forward, rather reluctantly. He turned around again. 'I hope you know what I'm doing!' He stepped into the cave before he had a chance to think too hard about what he was doing.

There was total silence in the cave. Steven glanced around, then something hit him, hard. The invisible creature had jumped at him, flailing away. With a cry, Steven started to fight back, struggling to get a grip on the thing as it twisted and squirmed. Claws raked at him, and he strove to keep them from cutting him. Something like a beak smacked the side of his face. Steven felt bony ribs, and squeezed hard. The thing squalled, and struggled harder.

Steven staggered back out of the cave, fighting at the creature. Instantly, the Doctor and Sara leaped to help him. They each grabbed a handful of invisible flesh and bones, and dragged the creature away from Steven. With one accord, they tossed it into one of the pits of bubbling mud. The creature splattered into it, sank, and then exploded out again.

They had a very brief glimpse of it – thin, bony, with two long, clawed arms, feet like birds' claws, and a narrow head with a beak. It screamed, and dashed into the jungle, leaving a trail of mud behind it.

'How horrible!' Sara breathed.

Steven straightened his clothing. 'It wasn't any fun grabbing it,' he complained.

'Quiet!' the Doctor hissed, holding up his hands. They listened. All about them, the bushes were rustling, as invisible shapes moved through them. 'They're coming.'

The bushes parted as the Visian war party slipped into

147

the clearing, ready for their attack. Before they could move, though, the bushes shook again. Then, from behind the Visians, a burst of fire turned the atmosphere bright. Screaming, several of the Visians must have died under the withering fire. The remainder whirled and fled.

Before the Doctor, Steven and Sara could move, the Dalek patrol emerged from the undergrowth, their guns trained on the trio. The patrol leader moved slightly ahead of the rest.

'You will come with us,' it ordered.

As calmly as he was able, the Doctor glanced at his two young companions. 'I'm afraid, my friends,' he sighed, 'the Daleks have won.'

14

Desperate Measures

The Visians regrouped a short distance away, glaring towards the Daleks with hatred and fear in almost equal parts in their hearts. Matters had seemed bad enough when the three strange intruders had appeared earlier. Three more mouths competing for the scarce food was bad enough, but at least those creatures had not killed anyone. The new arrivals – the metallic beings – had slain several of the Visians already. To the frightened, invisible creatures, this clearly meant only one thing: the latest arrivals were intending to take over the whole foraging area by wiping out the tribe!

The leader of the Visians whispered its instructions about. They were naturally a quiet people, since loud voices would have offset the advantages given them by their invisibility. 'We will surround these new invaders,' it hissed. 'Then we shall attack them and destroy them!'

The gathered Visians took up the quiet, intent refrain: 'Attack! Attack! Attack!'

The Dalek patrol leader moved forward slightly, and faced the old man, the ringleader of the thieves. 'You will hand over the Taranium core,' it ordered.

The Doctor raised an eyebrow, and sneered down his nose at the Dalek. He had beaten the Daleks many times in the past, and he refused to admit that they might really have won. He had spoken earlier only to prevent their opening fire on his companions. Gripping his lapels, he said: 'And if I do – what guarantee do I have that you won't shoot us down immediately afterwards?'

'There is no guarantee!' the Dalek grated.

The Dalek with the perceptor moved forwards, its device pointing directly at the Doctor and registering strongly. 'This one is carrying the Taranium core.'

'You will give it to us,' the patrol leader commanded.

'Doctor,' Sara cried, stepping towards him. 'Don't!'

The Dalek's eye-stick swung around to cover her. 'Silence! You will not speak.'

The Doctor stepped forwards, shielding both Steven and Sara to some degree. 'You cannot fire,' he said, smugly. 'You may damage the Taranium. As a way of ending this stalemate, might I suggest . . .'

'There will be no further discussion,' the Dalek snapped. It swung to indicate Steven and Sara. 'These two are of no consequence. Destroy them!'

The Daleks began to spread out about the three travellers, bringing their weapons to bear. The Doctor's mind raced, trying to think of some way out of this situation. Both Steven and Sara backed away slightly, trying to see some avenue of escape that the Daleks had overlooked. There was none.

Suddenly, a whispering, frantic horde of sticks and stones came hurtling down towards the Daleks. The Visians had built up their courage while the Daleks' attention was elsewhere. They rushed into the attack, screeching, and smashing with whatever they could lay their hands on.

Taken by surprise, the Daleks spun round to counterattack. One Dalek's eye-stick was smashed. Panicking, it began firing random bursts, yelling: 'Cannot see! Cannot see!' Most of the rocks and sticks did little damage, however, beyond denting the Dalek casings somewhat. Invisible claws grappled at the Daleks, and one was dragged by three Visians into a pool of the viscous mud, and pushed into it, face down. With a foul stench of escaping gases, the Dalek sank from sight.

'The invisible creatures must be exterminated!' the patrol leader ordered, rather unnecessarily, since the Daleks had already begun firing. 'They must not be allowed to interfere!'

Seizing their chance, the Doctor, Sara and Steven dashed

150

off into the jungle. The Visians must have seen them, but had correctly identified the Daleks as the greater danger, to be settled first.

The battle was very short-lived. The Daleks simply moved together into a tight circle, their guns facing outwards. They then began to fire heavy bursts in all directions. Screams and the crash of falling bodies proved that the Visians were suffering heavy losses. Finally, the few demoralized survivors fled into the jungle.

'Cease firing,' the patrol leader ordered.

'They have been driven off,' the perceptor Dalek observed. 'Or exterminated.'

'Search for the fugitives,' the leader responded. 'They have no means of escape from this planet. They must be annihilated!'

Breaking into small groups, the Daleks began to fan out from the clearing, searching for traces of the escaped captives.

Fighting to regain their breath, Sara, Steven and the Doctor had paused some distance away. They heard no signs of pursuit as yet. 'Can't hear anything now,' Sara gasped.

'It was a quick battle,' Steven replied grimly. 'I think we all know who won.'

The Doctor nodded, clutching at his side as he struggled to regain his composure. 'Yes, the Daleks will be following our trail. If we want to get away from this planet, we must move very fast – very fast indeed!' He started off again.

Sara glanced at Steven, puzzled. 'How *do* we get off this planet?' He shrugged; the Doctor would let them know his plan in his own sweet time. Till then, all they could do was to follow him.

It was quite intolerable. The Black Dalek glared down at the communications area with increased disgust. A servitor moved forward. The Black Dalek snapped: 'Are the fugitives still avoiding the Dalek patrols?'

'Yes. There has been no further contact with them.'

'Their recapture is simply a matter of time,' the Black

Dalek stated. 'There is no avenue of escape for them from Mira!' Though certain that this was true, the fact that the thieves of the core had already eluded capture on two other worlds gave the Black Dalek pause. These three humans were not typical of their species. Few had ever lived so long with such a pursuit force after them. It was as if they were used to the Dalek methods – and that was surely impossible! Humans had had no contact with the Daleks now for several centuries, and humans could not survive such a length of time. They could not know the Dalek ways – could they?

Exactly as the Doctor had suspected, the Dalek saucer lay in another of the small clearings. The heavy casings of the Daleks had sunk several inches into the Miran mud, and the trail had been simple to backtrack to this point. Hidden in the bushes, the three travellers peered out at the Dalek ship. It was a classic saucer shape, with a raised dome. Below, the ship stood on long legs. A central pod hung below the body, the exit door still open. From the door, a ramp led to the ground.

At the top of the ramp stood a Dalek guard.

The Doctor chuckled to himself, and gestured. 'There seems to be only *one* Dalek guard!'

Sara nodded, thoughtfully. 'So we take their ship to escape!' she breathed in admiration. 'Right, the best way to do it is to rush that guard from three sides at once.'

'Huh!' Steven snorted. 'Best way!'

Before Sara could retort, the Doctor held up a cautioning hand. 'Steven's right, my dear. There's a far better way. That Dalek could shoot us all down before we got anywhere near it. I have a plan. Just remember that the Dalek sees through that eye-stick on the top of its dome, and it cannot react faster than that stick can move! Now, Steven, this is what I want you to do . . .'

The Doctor hastily outlined his plan for the others. When he was certain that they had grasped it, he nodded, and moved off through the bushes. Sara glanced at Steven, unhappy over the plan.

'I don't like it,' she admitted. 'I still favour a frontal attack.'

'That's because you've not dealt with the Daleks before,' he answered. 'We have no option but to follow the Doctor's plans. He knows what he's doing.' Privately, Steven hoped that the Doctor really *did* know what he was doing . . .

The guard Dalek moved slowly backwards and forwards at the top of the ramp, awaiting the return of the patrol, or fresh instructions. It had been doing this for several hours, patiently, and nothing had happened. Suddenly, its sensors located something moving.

It looked around, and saw the elderly human move slowly from the trees. The creature did not seem to be armed in any way, but the Dalek levelled its gun in case. 'Remain where you are!' it commanded.

'Certainly,' the Doctor agreed cheerfully. He considered raising his arms, but that was such a tiring position in which to stand. Instead, he let them fall to his side, clearly empty. 'I have come to give myself up.'

The Dalek glided down the ramp towards him, cautiously. 'Are you the being with the Taranium core?'

'I am,' the Doctor replied. 'I realized how foolish I was being, that I am naturally no match for the Daleks. I will give you back the core, in exchance for your taking myself and my friends away from this wretched world.'

The Dalek examined the Doctor, thoughtfully. What the alien had said made perfect sense to it. The mention of the friends reminded the Dalek that there were two more of the aliens. 'Where are the others?' it asked.

Gesturing behind himself, the Doctor said: 'Over here, in the bushes. They will come when I call.'

Again, this was logical – but still the guard was suspicious. Why had the human so suddenly come to its senses? Was there some kind of trickery involved? It started to scan the bushes, slowly turning its head to do so. The Doctor began to sweat, because Steven was creeping up from behind the Dalek, a handful of mud ready to be used as a weapon. If the Dalek spun about much more . . .

'Here!' the Doctor said, suddenly, reaching towards his pocket. 'I will give you the Taranium core.'

At this, the Dalek's attention returned firmly to the Doctor, much to Steven's relief. The Doctor drew out the box containing the core, and held it slightly out.

'Do you wish me to hand it to you?' he asked, smiling his most beatific smile. 'Or would you rather I took it aboard your ship, mmm?'

The guard considered the matter. 'You will wait there until the patrol returns,' it decided. 'Tell the others to join you. If you make any attempt to escape . . .'

'Escape?' the Doctor interrupted, waving the thought airily away. 'You seem to forget that we came here and surrendered of our own free will!'

At that moment, Steven was close enough. He leaped for the Dalek, his hand slapping the mud over the eye-stick. The Dalek's head swivelled as it sought blindly for the source of the attack. Steven gave it a push, spinning the body so that if it fired, it would not hit the Doctor. Then he sprinted after the Doctor and Sara up the Dalek boarding ramp.

'Halt!' the guard screamed. 'Halt!' It fired, randomly, in a number of directions. It had no way of telling what – if anything – it was hitting, but this was all that it could do.

'Cease firing!' the patrol leader ordered, as it emerged from the jungle with the rest of the Daleks. 'Otherwise we will sustain damage.'

Obediently, the guard stopped. 'The fugitives are aboard the pursuit ship,' it informed its superior.

The patrol leader needed no further information. 'Board the ship!' it ordered the patrol. 'Exterminate the fugitives!'

The Doctor knew how lucky they were that the Daleks were such remorselessly logical beings. Their control boards were always laid out along much the same lines. He could not read their peculiar, angular script, but had no need to. He had examined a number of Dalek installations and craft during his numerous encounters with them, and was fairly familiar with the design that he faced now.

154

Though some of the Daleks possessed mechanical claws on their arm-sticks, most of them were fitted with the suction-cup devices instead. To adapt to those, the Dalek panels were always either touch or light activated. After a few nerve-racking seconds, the Doctor managed to unscramble the design of the control board. He began to power up the ship, building up the drive as fast as he dared.

'Hurry, Doctor!' Sara urged.

He nodded, his fingers flying over the control panels. Steven glanced out of the nearest viewport, and stiffened.

'There are Daleks all around us!' he exclaimed.

'Then close the hatch!' the Doctor snapped. He indicated a small panel by the open door. Sara dashed over, and hit the circular control. The hatch slid closed, cutting off both sight and sound of the Daleks.

The power was humming fiercely through the ship now, and the Doctor called out: 'Brace yourselves!' There were no couches for them to use, since the Daleks had no need for them. Instead, both Sara and Steven grabbed hold of panels to steady themselves. The Doctor nodded, and manipulated the final controls.

On the planet's surface, the Daleks ground to a halt, then retreated. Their ship shuddered, lifted slowly at first, then shot upwards at a tremendous pace, until it was a faint light in the sky.

The patrol leader looked back down, at its second in command. 'Contact the planet Kembel,' it ordered. 'We must report this to the Dalek Supreme!'

The control room on Kembel was its usual orderly, efficiently running place when Mavic Chen stepped into it. Seeing the Black Dalek by the tracking devices, Chen moved over towards that section, without hurrying. The Daleks ignored his presence until he stood by the Black Dalek.

'I have returned from Earth,' Chen began, 'as I consider . . .'

'Mavic Chen,' the Dalek interrupted, 'you have failed in your task.'

'Failed?' Chen looked shocked. 'Is this my greeting?' He spread his hands. 'I agree that my mission was to return to Earth and recover the Taranium. This I have not done . . .'

'Failure,' the Black Dalek grated, 'will not be tolerated.'

'*But*,' Chen continued, smoothly, 'I did notify you of the whereabouts of the fugitives.' He indicated the lit star maps beyond them. 'The planet Mira. There, the vital core can be taken from them without suspicion. Their presence on the Earth was a constant danger – at any time they might have contacted forces unsympathetic to our plans. I had to get them off the Earth as soon as I could.'

The Black Dalek did not believe this for a second. He knew of Chen's glib tongue, and the snares and lies it could create. 'You make your incompetence sound like an achievement!'

This was too much for the Guardian, hitting him in his weakest point – his ego. Instead of controlling himself, he growled back: '*Incompetence*? Incompetence now, is it? You seem to have forgotten that the original blunder was not of my doing. I journeyed to and from the Earth to correct a failing that *your* security force should have dealt with. The core was stolen from *here*! My actions have brought about a situation which will allow you to recover the Taranium core with ease. If *that* is a failure – then I have failed.' He glared at the Black Dalek, daring it to repeat its accusation.

Instead, it turned towards another Dalek that had been edging forward, trying to get attention. 'Report!'

The communications Dalek said: 'The fugitives have stolen our pursuit ship.'

What perfect timing! Mavic Chen thought, and a smile of superiority and contempt crossed his features as he looked contemptuously at the Black Dalek. The message had underscored his speech as if it had been timed.

Ignoring Chen for the moment, the Black Dalek asked the communications Dalek: 'Have they left the planet Mira?'

'Yes. Their course is being computed.'

'What of our force?'

'They are stranded on the planet. They are under constant attack from the invisible inhabitants of Mira.'

The Black Dalek considered. 'Leave them,' it finally ordered. 'They have failed the Daleks. I will supervise the recovery of the Taranium myself.'

'I obey.' The messenger returned to its duties.

Chen moved forward again, smiling with amusement. 'And you had the audacity to accuse me, Mavic Chen, of incompetence!' he crowed. 'A Dalek pursuit ship . . . stolen! *Really!*'

The human was beginning to annoy the Black Dalek. 'It is not an emergency,' it responded.

'No,' Chen agreed. 'More like a catastrophe!'

Such arrogance from a human! The Black Dalek chose its words carefully. 'They may believe that they have successfully escaped from us. But we are in control at all times.' Turning its back on Chen, the Supreme Dalek moved away down the room. Puzzled, Chen stared after it. Obviously, then, the Daleks still had a trick or two up their metallic sleeves!

The Dalek pursuit ship was fairly large, and well laid out. Beyond the control room, the travellers had discovered a well-equipped laboratory, a store room and several rooms that were clearly where the Daleks rested between duties. Emptying out three of the cases in the store room had yielded them something to sit on at least. The Doctor had laid a course for Earth into the computers, which were busily running the ship.

The Doctor had seated himself in the laboratory, and fished the Taranium core from his pocket. Using the instrumentation he had found, he began to examine the core minutely, and measure it carefully. Steven and Sara, not too interested in this, were carrying on a somewhat strained conversation.

'So,' Sara asked him, 'what do *you* think we should do then, Steven?'

'I don't know,' he replied hotly. 'I've been trying to figure it out. It seems crazy to try to get back to Kembel;

the Daleks are sure to be waiting for us there. But that's where the TARDIS is.'

'Your machine that travels through space and time?' she replied, mocking him. What a story he had told her – that he was from her past, and the Doctor from some strange world that he never spoke of, and that they roamed the dimensions in a strange ship called a TARDIS. 'I find it hard to believe that such a craft exists.'

'I don't much care what you think,' Steven retorted. 'We just have to get it back again before the Daleks discover what it is.'

'But you said that you've met the Daleks before. Don't they recognize this TARDIS, then?'

'They might not,' Steven answered. 'You see, we don't always know exactly *when* we land when we land. Maybe this is earlier in time than when I first met them and they had a time machine too. In that case, maybe they don't know about the TARDIS yet.'

'That's a lot of maybes,' Sara answered. 'Still, it's all irrelevant to me. My duty is clear – to work on the destruction of the Dalek invasion forces.' She looked at him very carefully. 'And I won't let anything stand in my way.'

Steven felt chilled. 'You don't have to paint a picture.' He knew she would kill both him and the Doctor if she felt that they were endangering her mission. Or – would she? Certainly, when they had first met her, she would have slaughtered them without hesitation. But now . . . now she knew them better, and he had half an idea that she admired the Doctor. Maybe she even liked him? Could she be so coldly efficient now and kill them?

He moved away, and walked into the laboratory. The Doctor glanced up and smiled.

'Ah, Steven, good.' He passed over a pad and stylus. 'Take this down, will you?'

Still looking back at Sara, Steven took the pad, not really paying attention. She was standing in the control room, staring out at the stars. What was going through her head? Was she certain she would do anything to further her cause? Or was she beginning to admit that she had human feelings, that she could actually get to be fond of people? She was a very good-looking woman, and Steven couldn't help but wonder if she could ever unbend enough to become romantic. He became suddenly aware that the Doctor had said something, and was looking expectantly up at him. Hastily, Steven stammered, 'We're still on course, Doctor.'

'Yes, yes, no doubt we are,' the Doctor agreed. 'Now, stop day-dreaming and pay attention. Take this down.' He returned to his examination of the core. 'Energy ratio point 003. Carbon scan – 2795. Variable rate at . . .' He broke off, aware that Steven hadn't written a word, but was looking back at Sara again. He snorted to himself. What was it about youth that made young humans so disposed to moon over members of the opposite sex? 'I'll do it if you're going to day-dream.'

Steven dragged his attention back, and became aware of the pad and stylus. 'No, it's all right. What were you saying? Something about carbon?' He ignored the Doctor's withering glare. 'What are we doing anyway?' he added.

'*We?*' the Doctor growled. 'My dear boy, *I* am attempting to make a copy of the core. It has to be good enough to fool the Daleks. They're not going to stop hunting us until they have recovered the core – or what they *think* is the core.'

Catching on, Steven grinned. 'And we're . . . *you're* . . .' he corrected hastily as the Doctor glared at him. 'You're going to see that they get a useless copy.'

'It's worth a try,' the Doctor said, modestly. 'It might just buy us breathing space.'

The vibrations under the floor suddenly began to change their tempo. Puzzled, they looked at each other, then moved back to the control room. It was obvious that something was changing, because the stars were altering their positions out of the ports.

Sara looked up from the panel. 'We're moving off a direct course,' she reported.

Annoyed, the Doctor moved forward, brushing her aside. 'I do wish you wouldn't touch things!' he snapped.

'I *didn't!*' Sara retorted.

One glance at the panel confirmed that. 'Yes, I believe

you, my dear.' The Doctor studied the board. Parts of it were now dead when he tried to reset it. Another whole panel had lit up, and was showing impulses playing all over it. Gesturing to the panel, he said: 'I'm afraid the ship is under Dalek influence.'

'They're piloting us by remote control?' asked Steven.

'Yes, my boy – and we're now on a course for the planet Kembel . . .'

15

Out Of Time

Steven regarded the panel controlling their destiny for a moment. Then he walked into the laboratory and picked up a length of piping. Returning to the control room, he brought the piping down on the remote control unit. It exploded, showering glassite and components about the room. With evident satisfaction, Steven smiled at the smoking ruins.

Finally, Sara spoke. 'Isn't that rather an abrupt way of dealing with the problem?'

Steven had had quite enough of her. 'Look, my technology may be a couple of hundred years behind yours and the Doctor's, but there are still some things I can handle.'

The Doctor raised an eyebrow. 'I would say in rather a – ah – terminal fashion,' he chuckled. 'Let's see if we can take control of our destiny again, shall we?' He crossed to the main controls, and started to experiment. To his immense satisfaction, they reponded instantly. 'Well, it seems as though drastic measures do sometimes pay off, eh, my boy?'

'Yes.' Steven looked down at the smoking, sparking ruin of the panel. 'I wonder what the Daleks will do next?'

'The control beam has been broken,' the monitor Dalek reported.

'Understood,' the Black Dalek replied. It spun about to another of the many control boards in the room. 'Activate the magnetized beam.'

The Daleks at this unit had anticipated the command, and had the systems powered. On the instructions, they began to focus their instruments. 'Pursuit ship held on magnetized beam,' one finally reported.

'Speed constant,' the second added. 'Fourteen degrees deviation.'

'Estimated time of arrival,' said the third, 'four units.'

Mavic Chen looked towards the Black Dalek. 'I sincerely hope that there will be no further bungling . . .'

The Black Dalek's eye-stick spun to focus on him, obviously annoyed at this remark. 'The fugitives will be exterminated upon arrival.'

'*After* we have the Taranium core in our possession,' Chen added.

The Black Dalek regarded him coldly. It seemed as though the human was having difficulty recalling his place in all of this. If it was not that he was still useful to the Daleks, he would be dead by now. The Black Dalek relished the thought of what he would do when Chen was no longer valuable . . .

Having solved their problems with the Dalek control, the travellers had all returned to the laboratory. Together, they had helped the Doctor to construct his imitation core. Finally, wiping the sweat from his brow with a large bandanna, the Doctor held up his forgery. 'There you are,' he said, pleased with himself. 'What do you think of it?'

Sara took it from the Doctor, and began to examine it from all angles. Steven peered over her shoulder and grinned. 'Very good, Doctor,' he approved. 'It looks exactly the same.'

'Yes,' Sara admitted, doubtfully. 'But as soon as you touch it, you can tell it's not Taranium. There's no charge in it, no glow, no life. If you touch the other core, there's a sort of shock . . .'

The Doctor nodded, and took back the fake core. 'I know, my dear. The way I have built this, it will take only an influx of energy to bring it to life.'

'How will you activate it?' Steven asked.

The Doctor looked slightly embarrassed. 'Ah, that's the

part of the plan I'm still working on. It will need a tremendous input of energy.'

Steven grinned, certain he had the answer to the problem. 'We could use the gravity force from the ship's power banks,' he suggested. He was sure they could easily rig a drain, and have the core powered up in moments. The Doctor and Sara evidently didn't share his confidence in his solution, for they exchanged grave looks. 'Well,' Steven asked, defensively, 'what's wrong with that?'

The Doctor patted him condescendingly on the shoulder. 'Too primitive, my boy, too primitive – and far too dangerous.'

Sara added: 'Gravity force as a source of energy was abandoned centuries ago.'

Feeling hot in the face, Steven snapped back: '*We* were still using it.' His own century had refined the flow of gravitic energy to power starships, to light cities and to defy the bounds of gravity; it was the energy system that Steven knew best, and he didn't want to admit that controlling it was at all dangerous. His pride wouldn't allow him.

'Oh yes?' Sara said, sweetly. 'And the Romans used treadmills. I don't think that would do the job, either.' She and the Doctor ignored him, and began sketching out a circuit diagram that Sara felt they could adapt from the ship's energies to do the task.

Sulkily, Steven turned away from them, and kicked at a scrap of machinery on the floor. 'I still think gravity force would do the trick,' he muttered to himself. He hated to admit it, but he was feeling very useless at the moment. When he had first joined the Doctor, he had been the one from the most advanced society – after the Doctor himself, naturally – and he had been able to act like an older brother to Vicki. She had been from a time a few hundred years before his – almost prehistoric, as far as he was concerned. Now he knew how Vicki must have felt at times. Sara was a few centuries ahead of him in technology, and he didn't understand half of the concepts she and the Doctor were tossing back and forth.

The ship lurched again, and the stars began to shift once

more. Sara glanced up from the table in alarm. 'We're changing course again!' She and the Doctor left the fake core on the laboratory table and dashed back to the control room. The Doctor began examining the instruments there, and shook his head in annoyance.

'Dear, dear, dear,' he murmured. 'We're caught in a very highly concentrated magnetic beam of some kind.' He didn't have to say where it was originating.

Sara looked at him with concern etched into her pretty face. 'This course will take us right back to the Daleks!'

Alone in the laboratory, Steven glared at Sara and the Doctor. They were huddling down again, talking together, and he was left out. Moodily, he kicked the circuit on the floor again. 'Primitive!' he grunted. Then he saw the core, and an idea lit up his eyes. He glanced at the Doctor and Sara, who were fussing over the controls now. They would be busy for the few minutes that it would take . . .

He went to the wall panel, and traced the feed lines for the gravitic energy the Daleks were using for the ship's artificial gravity field. Once he was certain he had the right lines, he clipped in two extension wires, and a transformer to step down the power. The other end of this he connected to the fake core. 'Let's see how primitive I am now!' he muttered to himself in satisfaction. By the time that the other two had finished fiddling with the controls, he'd have the core all powered up to show them what he could do. He threw the final connections to his apparatus.

A tremendous shock passed right through him, as the gravitic power suddenly altered its flow. He screamed, a distorted, echoing cry of pain, as blackness closed in about him. The wiring melted, the transformer shorted and exploded.

In the control room, the floor seemed to lurch, due to the drained gravity field. After a nauseous second, the field stabilized again, and Sara and the Doctor heard Steven's cry. They dashed into the laboratory, and saw Steven. He was standing, looking vaguely shocked.

'My dear boy,' the Doctor asked in alarm, 'what's happened?'

Seeing the melted connections and the still smouldering transformer, Sara knew. 'The fool! He's charged the core with gravitic lines of power! And we warned him!'

Steven's lack of response bothered the Doctor far more at the moment. He waved a hand in front of his young friend's eyes, without eliciting any response at all. 'He's still alive,' he said. 'But . . .' He reached to try to take Steven's pulse. His fingers met resistance a few inches away from Steven's wrist. Puzzled, he tried again for the other arm. Again, he felt a strange effect when he came within a couple of inches of Steven, and could move his hand no closer. He began to test the air all about the young man, and discovered that this field of force about him extended between an inch and two inches all over Steven's body. Obviously, though, air was getting through to him, since the Doctor could see the rise and fall of his companion's chest.

'Doctor!' Sara interrupted his examination, grabbing his arm and pointing to the fake core. 'It worked! It's just like the real Taranium!'

Indeed it was: the imitation glowed with the same eerie light as the real core that was in the Doctor's pocket. The same strange energy forces flowed across it – or, at least, *appeared* to flow across it. The Doctor smiled, tightly. 'That's wonderful,' he admitted. 'Steven's theory has proved successful. But – Steven himself . . .'

Sara followed his worried gaze back to Steven. The young man was standing, his eyes open and unfocused, breathing gently. There was no sign of intelligence behind the eyes at all.

The activity in the Dalek central control on Kembel was at its height. The magnetic grappling beam that the Daleks were using to drag back their pursuit ship drew a great deal of power from their reserves. This drain was being carefully monitored, while the focus of the beam was being kept tight. Various ranks of Daleks were in constant motion.

'The pursuit ship has entered the atmosphere,' the monitor controller reported.

'Reducing speed,' added the scanning Dalek. 'Ten degrees of light speed. Eight. Six . . .'

'Landing area has been computed,' the monitor said. 'Sector seven.'

The Black Dalek noted these figures, then turned to Mavic Chen, who was peering eagerly at the instruments. 'The Dalek forces are moving into position.'

Chen nodded. 'It appears that you've at last succeeded in getting the Taranium back.'

Again, that arrogance! 'Of course,' the Black Dalek stated. 'And we shall deal with these fugitives as we deal with all who oppose the Daleks.'

Thoughtfully, Chen shook his head. 'No.'

The Black Dalek didn't like that at all. 'Do you challenge us?' it grated.

'Oh, no,' Chen lied, glibly. 'But might it not be advisable for me to take them back to Earth for a public trial and execution?'

'Why?'

'Some people on Earth know that the traitors were transported to Mira,' Chen explained. 'If they simply disappear, those people might become curious as to what happened to them. It's possible that they might then uncover some portion of our plans.'

'It is essential that you do not allow your Earth people to become curious,' the Black Dalek replied, flatly.

'Human curiosity is something I can have no control over!' Chen protested.

'You must forestall their questions until it is too late.' The Black Dalek spun about, but its eye-stick remained focused on the human. 'We shall have conquered the Solar System before our involvement is suspected.'

'It is possible,' Chen agreed.

'Once we have the Taranium, there is nothing to stop us!' The Black Dalek was convinced of this. 'The Time Destructor is here, and we shall have the power that we have worked for! The Daleks will be supreme!'

This was the information that Chen had been fishing for. The Time Destructor was already here! Excellent. He nodded. 'Very well,' he agreed, condescendingly. 'I will leave their fate to you.' He nodded at the tracking station. 'The Dalek reception committee should be in place now. I think it's about time we left to join them, don't you?'

The Black Dalek regarded Chen once again. This human was getting more presumptuous as time went by! He would need to be dealt with shortly. For now, though – patience! Turning, the Dalek Supreme led the way out of the control room. The Taranium was almost recovered. This time, nothing could go wrong!

Sara glanced out of the portal, worried. Kembel filled the entire viewing area, and she could pick out the continents, rivers and lakes without any trouble at all. 'We're losing height fast,' she observed. 'Just a few minutes to touchdown.'

The Doctor seemed to be paying no attention to this at all. He was still examining Steven, clucking to himself in annoyance. 'Dear, dear, dear. I have no idea how we can cure this condition of his.' He glanced over at Sara. 'He seems conscious, but his mental processes have slowed somewhat. Air is reaching him, and so is light. Possibly sound. Yet his mind seems in the grip of some form of paralysis from this field.' He looked back at Steven. 'Raise your left hand, my boy.' Mechanically, Steven did as he was told, and then lowered it at the Doctor's command. 'He's like an automaton. Everything functions, but his will is not making any connection with his body.'

'How horrible,' Sara said. 'He's neither alive nor dead. Entombed in a force field.'

The Doctor nodded. 'But there has to be some solution – there has to be!'

The craft rocked as it entered the buffeting of the atmosphere. The Doctor joined Sara at the controls. 'We're slowing,' he observed. 'Coming in for a landing. Brace yourself!'

Standing in the clearing, Chen looked into the night sky with a good deal of satisfaction. One of the lights in the sky was growing progressively brighter – the ship was being dragged down precisely on target! In a matter of minutes, the Taranium core would be in his hands again, and he would be on his way to Universal domination . . .

The ship grew larger in the sky, blanking out the stars. The pressure of the air whipped up a wind that washed over Chen, tugging his clothing and hair. The Daleks, naturally, seemed unaffected by this. Finally, gently, the pursuit ship touched down. Its legs bit into the ground, and it stood there in the burned-out remnants of the forest.

The Black Dalek turned to the patrol leader. 'Inform the city that the magnetic beam is to be discontinued. They are to drain the ship's power to prevent it from taking off again.'

'I obey.'

Chen smiled and rubbed his hands together in satisfaction. 'It would appear that everything is progressing according to plan,' he observed.

'The Taranium core will be recovered,' the Black Dalek stated. 'This time, there will be no errors.'

Chen inclined his head slightly. 'Let us hope that you are right.'

Sara held the fake Taranium core carefully. It glowed and pulsed with life, just like its real counterpart – which was securely nestled in the Doctor's inside pocket. She looked from the false core to the Doctor. 'But it won't – it *can't* work!' She was afraid that the Daleks would somehow sense the substitution that the Doctor had been carefully planning.

He dismissed her fears with a wave of his hand. 'It's our only chance, my dear.' He had improvised another of his brilliant plans in the final moments before landing, and had every confidence it would work perfectly. 'Now, remember – I will do all the talking.' He turned to the expressionless Steven. 'Listen carefully, my boy, and do exactly what I tell you, ummm? Now, come along – follow me!'

He led the way to the exit port. The Daleks undoubtedly had some way of getting into the ship, so it was best to forestall their attack by apparent compliance. Steven followed him, stopping when he stopped. Looking very worried, Sara brought up the rear. Nodding, the Doctor hit the sensor plate, and the airlock door hissed open.

The Daleks were waiting, standing in a circle about the ramp. Also there, by the Black Dalek, was the tall, distinguished frame of Mavic Chen. The Dalek guns were all focused on the doorway. The Doctor held his hand out to Sara, and she passed him the fake core. Holding this prominently before himself, the Doctor slowly walked down the ramp. The guns followed him, but none of the Daleks opened fire.

As he reached the bottom of the ramp, Chen stepped forward. 'Is that the Taranium core?' he asked, rather unnecessarily. He were merely establishing for the Doctor that he was in command here – not the Daleks.

'Yes.'

Chen reached out his hand. 'Then I would suggest that you give it to me.'

The Doctor shook his head, firmly. 'No.'

Chen's sweep of an arm took in all of the Dalek forces about them. 'Come, now, you are beyond help. Be reasonable.'

'You dare not fire,' the Doctor replied. 'You might damage the core.'

'Possibly,' Chen conceded. 'On the other hand, you are not in any secure position from which to bargain.'

'I will hand over the Taranium,' the Doctor agreed, slowly. 'Outside my ship, the TARDIS – or nowhere!'

Chen cocked his head on one side, and considered the point. So that strange, blue box that had survived the burning of the jungle belonged to this old man? Was that how he and it had got here? It seemed to be a fairly innocent request. Even if the Doctor got into it, he could hardly lift off without the Daleks dragging him back with their magnetic devices. Chen turned to the Black Dalek, and gestured it to follow him out of earshot of the Doctor. 'You heard his conditions?'

'Yes,' the Black Dalek agreed. 'We do not negotiate.'

'He seems very determined,' Chen replied. 'Does it really matter where we get the core?'

The Black Dalek wondered if Chen had a hand in this somehow after all. The Earth female was one of his agents, and the other two seemed to be human – though there was something familiar about the older man. 'His extermination is inevitable wherever the hand-over is made.'

Chen spread his hands. 'Then may I suggest that we humour him and allow him the choice of where he is to die?'

'Very well,' the Black Dalek agreed. 'In front of his ship.'

They moved back to join the Doctor. Chen smiled happily at the Doctor, who was not taken in by him for a second. He was well aware of what the human and Dalek had been planning. Chen gestured for the Doctor to follow. 'As you wish,' he said, 'we will take possession of the Taranium at your ship.'

The Doctor nodded, keeping a firm grip on the fake core. He turned to Steven and Sara. 'Come along, both of you,' he said, softly. 'And stay close to me.'

As they started off, the Daleks keeping their distance, but ever alert. Chen finally caught sight of the girl with the old man. Could it be possible to use her again, he wondered. 'Kingdom . . .' he began.

Sara turned her eyes on him. When he had last seen them, they appeared emotionless, calm and efficient. Now he saw hatred and loathing in them. 'Traitor!' she hissed. She had to restrain herself from leaping at him. Chen backed away slightly. Well, she would obviously be of no help to him.

He moved to join the old man. 'Well,' he said, pleasantly, 'you've led us a merry chase across half a Galaxy, haven't you? I should like at least to know your name.'

The Doctor looked at him. He had nothing but contempt for anyone who thought they could ally themselves with the Daleks – especially one who was as trusted as Chen was. 'I am glad to have caused you so much trouble,' he said, coldly. 'And perhaps may discomfort you still. I am known as the Doctor.'

The Black Dalek's eye-stick spun to focus on him. 'Doctor?' it repeated. The Dalek finally realized who this being was. This wandering time traveller had defeated the Daleks several times in the past, but the Black Dalek had never confronted him before – though it had ordered his extermination many times. Now it was apparent why there had been so many problems with securing the core. The Doctor was a master of confusion and planning. This time, however, the Daleks had out-thought their great foe!

The short walk had brought them to the TARDIS. It stood in the midst of the blackened stalks of the trees where the Doctor had left it – just a few days ago, but it seemed like months! The door was slightly ajar, as Katarina must have left it. Now Katarina was dead, and Bret Vyon was dead. Steven was mindless. Only the Doctor was unchanged by all that had happened. He had even gained a new companion, for at least the time being. Sara could not be left here to the Daleks and Mavic Chen. She would undoubtedly be killed.

The Doctor halted in front of the TARDIS, and called Steven to him. Steven obeyed, and held out his hands on command. The Doctor placed the fake core in his hands – actually, floating an inch or so above them – and then faced the Daleks and Chen.

'Sara, go into the ship,' he ordered. Though she couldn't understand why he'd want her inside that small box, she knew him enough to trust him, and did as she was told. 'Now,' the Doctor continued, speaking to Chen. 'The young man will give you the Taranium when I am safely inside my ship.'

Chen smiled, complacently. 'Making sure of your escape, eh, Doctor?' He could understand that well enough! It would be a futile hope, because the Dalek firepower would destroy the craft before it could move.

The Doctor didn't reply. Instead, he spoke urgently to Steven. 'Do exactly as I say, Steven. When I am inside the

TARDIS, you will hand the core to Mavic Chen, then come into the TARDIS. We shall wait for you.'

Glaring at the assembled Daleks and the patiently waiting Chen, the Doctor slipped into the TARDIS. Once he had done so, Steven took a step forward and held out the core. Chen grabbed for it, eagerly. The familiar shock of touching the core went through his arm.

'The core!' he gloated. 'At last!'

As he moved back, Steven turned to enter the TARDIS. The Black Dalek waited for Chen to dash aside, carrying the precious core, then its gun came up.

'Exterminate!'

The Dalek squad opened fire. Their deadly radiations bathed Steven, but he didn't fall. Instead, as the light died down, he shook his head, glanced about and dashed into the TARDIS. The door slammed closed behind him.

'Fire!' The Black Dalek ordered, and the Daleks all blasted away at the craft. Their weapons had no effect, and the TARDIS began to wheeze and groan. The light on its top started to flash and rotate. Slowly, it faded from sight, until it had totally vanished.

'Our weapons did not take effect,' the Black Dalek stated.

'All were operating at full power,' the patrol leader reported. There had been no malfunctions, yet . . .

'It is not possible that the human could live through that,' the Black Dalek said.

Mavic Chen wasn't interested in that. It meant little to him whether the Doctor and his two friends lived or died. 'What happened is unimportant!' he exclaimed, studying the core with joy. 'We have the Taranium core! The invasion can go ahead. *The Universe will be ours!*'

16

Interlude

Sara was dumbfounded at the size of the room she was in. The TARDIS was so large inside, yet so small from the outside. She was standing by a control panel in the centre of the spacious room, watching the rise and fall of a rotor of some kind. The Doctor straightened up from the controls, and glanced over at Steven, who had collapsed into a stately, tall-backed chair after he had dashed inside.

Crossing to the chair, Sara looked down at the young man in some concern. 'Are you sure that you're all right?'

Shaking a little after the ordeal, Steven was happy just to be able to experience his body again. 'Yes. It was so weird . . . as if I were watching myself move, but without any way to affect it. I could see and hear, but nothing I could do made any difference, until the second that the Daleks fired at me. Then I was back to normal, and inside the ship like a shot!'

The Doctor joined them, chuckling to himself. 'The Dalek guns must have destroyed that force-field around you completely. Its effects were loosened, and you came to. You're just lucky that they didn't fire on you a second time, eh?'

Steven didn't even want to think about that. He climbed to his feet and walked – somewhat unsteadily – to the mushroom-shaped control panel. 'We're on our way, then?'

'Where to?' Sara asked. 'We should try to return to Kembel and find some way to disable their fleet.'

The Doctor shook his head. 'There's very little chance of that, my dear. This old ship of mine has its own ideas about where we're heading, you know. We could never make it back to Kembel in the same time period that you are from.'

He took the real core from his pocket, and held it up. 'Besides, as long as the Daleks never get hold of this, the Galaxy is safe.'

'Or,' Steven amended, 'they can meet the Daleks in a fair fight, and combat them with all of the vast science at their disposal. They won't have to worry about the Daleks using a Time Destructor.'

Sara struggled to take in all of this. 'Then – Mavic Chen will go unpunished for what he has done?'

'I shouldn't think so,' the Doctor said, gently. 'He'll discover soon that the Daleks don't take allies – only victims. He'll over-reach himself, and they will kill him.'

'That's not really our concern any longer,' Steven said. 'We've beaten them – and the whole of time and space is open to us. Sara, you're in for some real fun!'

She dragged her mind away from thoughts of revenge, and looked carefully about the room. 'This really is a time and space machine?' she asked. 'It can go anywhere – any time?' She smiled at the thought. 'It's so . . . fantastic.'

'Yes,' laughed the Doctor. 'Isn't it? Steven, my boy, would you like to show Sara to Vicki's old room? I'm sure she'll feel better after a bath and a change of clothing.'

'A bath!' Sara said, closing her eyes in anticipation of the treat. 'That sounds marvellous.' When she opened her eyes, she caught sight of the Taranium core, perched on the control console. She suddenly sobered up. 'Doctor,' she asked, softly, 'what will the Daleks do when they find out they *don't* have the Taranium core?' She searched his face for an answer. 'What will they do then?'

The Doctor turned away from her. He stared at the blank monitor screen to avoid looking at his friends. 'Then,' he replied, 'they will try to find it – and us.'

'Can they do that?' Sara asked. 'Can they . . . follow us?'

'They did once,' the Doctor answered. 'Perhaps they can again – if they have to.'

The three of them turned to stare at the Taranium core. They had escaped the Daleks for now . . . but as long as it existed, there would always be the terrible possibility that one day they would encounter the Daleks again . . .

ARE YOU BUYING DOCTOR WHO MAGAZINE?

Every monthly issue of *Doctor Who Magazine* is packed with information about the world's longest running SF television programme, including news, interviews, archives, and a brand new comic strip featuring the current Doctor! Special reports cover subjects such as visual effects, design, merchandise and reviews of all the new Target Books.

Subscribe to *Doctor Who Magazine* by filling out or copying the coupon below, enclosing a cheque for the appropriate amount (made payable to Marvel Comics Ltd.), to *Doctor Who Magazine* Subscriptions, P.O. Box 500, Leicester LE99 0AA.

Subscription rates as follows: United Kingdom £15.00; Overseas £25.00; US $45.00. Offer expires December 30th 1989; please allow 28 days for your subscription to take effect.

I would like to keep up to date on the worlds of *Doctor Who* and enclose a cheque/P.O./International Money Order for £15.00/£25.00/$45.00*, made payable to Marvel Comics Ltd., for a 12 issue subscription to *Doctor Who Magazine*.

*Delete as appropriate. Offer expires December 30th 1989.

Name ....

Address ....

....

....Age ....

TGT BKS